A CHALLENGE FROM THE PAST

"You got money?" Uncle Bad Knees asked.

"Plenty," said Badger.

"Time to pack." His uncle limped into the kitchen. "You follow their trail, stop at Mike's, I'll send him word."

"Uncle, you think they'll split up?"

"That breed? Can't stand their own smell long."

"Then how ... ?"

"Find where they split. Pick one, go after him, make him tell where the other went."

"Make him?"

"Same way they made your mother talk."

"Uncle, what kind of men ... ?"

"Don't care. Find them, kill them, bring me your mother's necklace. Then I'll know you done it."

Bantam Books by Frank O'Rourke

BADGER
THE SHOTGUN MAN

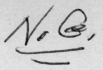

BADGER

Frank O'Rourke

BADGER
A Bantam Book / June 1977

ISBN 0–553–02146–X

Published simultaneously in the United States and Canada

PRINTED IN THE UNITED STATES OF AMERICA

1

People called him Badger, not curious enough to learn that badger was American for *blaireau*. Henri Blaireau, firstborn of an Indian mother and a French-Canadian father, mixed-blood in a simon-pure world. Often too early or too late, as on that cool autumn day at the Gregory depot, taking the southbound train, hearing of Standing Bear's death one week after the old chief was buried on the chalk bluff above the Missouri with unnumbered generations of ancestors, not to mention Badger's father and the other white men of the tribe's eighth clan. Badger dozed from Burke through Bonesteel, woke during the Monomi stop, saw the blue haze above the river bluffs, never sure it was smoke or weather until he sniffed, slept again, heard the conductor call "Swiftwater!" and found his youngest sister Amelie waiting on the platform in her black dress, face so sad he half-guessed before her words came in a tearful rush.

"Henry—Mother's dead!"

"But how can that be? She was fine when I left."

"Murdered!"

"Oh god—" he led her to the wagon, drove from town across the Swiftwater bridge on the reservation road that wound through the rounded hills sloping south from the Missouri bluffs into the frost-browned bottoms. Four miles from town the paints swung up the lane into the farmyard made small by teams and

1

wagons. His sisters Marie and Sophie, their husbands and children, his brother Pete and Nora, Amelie—all followed him into the house where Marie, next eldest, told how the entire tribe had gathered on the chalk bluff to bury the old chief and, after full honors were paid, their mother sent Amelie with Pete and Nora for a little visit and drove home alone. Two days later her dog Four-eyes came to Uncle Bad Knees' cabin and barked him back to the farm. He found her, drove to Ben Ore's, returned and waited until the tribal agent, the county sheriff, and all of them came. Missing from the torn-up house were thirty-one silver dollars and their mother's necklace. They redd up the house and began the four days mourning, hoped he'd get back in time, finally had to bury her beside their father on the chalk bluff. Now they were ready to go home, Uncle Bad Knees expected him.

"What about Amelie?"

"She stays with Pete and Nora."

Badger wanted desperately to be alone but they sat heavy as lead, even the children seemed to know that he was the blood vengeance man, they must all bid him a silent farewell. He went out to the wagon and drove north through the hills, Four-eyes leading the paints along the old trail to the cabin on the oak bluff. Four-eyes resembled a small collie but her strain of hunting dog had roots in tribal antiquity; black along the spine, neck, and top of the head, tan below, her breed got its name from the two creamy brown spots above the eyes. She trotted across the yard to the arbor and sat beside Uncle Bad Knees, tongue lolling, as if saying what a good thing I brought him, Uncle, he'd lose his ass in a muleyard; and his mother's oldest brother, lying against a willow rod lazyback, lifted his face of hammered iron oxidized by time, watershed cheeks eroded from that continental divide nose into a wattled neck brushed by the faded green ribbons plaited into his scraggy braids. He wore leggings, breech cloth, belt, and parfleche-soled moccasins over a body mostly skin, bone, and bad temper, eyes as brightly malicious as in Badger's youth when uncle taught nephew all the things nobody else knew he had learned. Harsh voice rasped from sunken chest:

"Sell your rotgut to those dumb Sioux?"

"Yes, Uncle."

"Put up your team."

Badger led the paints to the barn, forked hay and poured oats, returned to the arbor and lay against the visitor's lazyback, Four-eyes between them, all looking eastward through the oaks down the sweep of the river. His uncle's dusty, scrawny chickens sashayed past, roosters daring Four-eyes to come out and fight, hens cackling exultantly over eggs laid where foxes could not go; as mean and durable as the uncle taking his own dour time to remind the nephew of ancient tribal custom.

"You look for sign?"

"Came straight here, Uncle."

"That fatass sheriff kicked around, said rain washed out all the tracks. Blind fool! Four of them left a trail babies could follow. Tore up the house, busted things, smashed the animals—" his uncle meant the clay figures Badger had sculpted in childhood: bear, horses, dogs "—always liked that first dog."

"So did Mother."

"They hurt her, took her necklace, only thing she ever valued, killed her, ran. Two in a wagon, two on horses. Go look at the line."

Badger walked through the oaks to the ravine, toed his way down the zigzag path to water's edge, took a channel cat off the set line, cleaned it on the flat rock, scraped guts and skin into the current, washed his knife, carried the filets up the path into fresh-fallen darkness. The wind was talking, his uncle and Four-eyes had gone inside. Badger followed, built a fire in the stove, cooked the fish with squash, sat eating with his uncle. An admirer had brought the squash, two combs of honey, and a sack of black walnuts. The oily whiff of drying walnuts chased the yellow bake of squash through the fried fish into the time-absorbing cabin smell; eating calmly, insensible to decades of squash, walnuts, honey, fish, furs, hides, iron, gunpowder, flint, steel, sweat, raw meat, wet blood, and a hundred salves, his uncle spoke pensively between bites, naming every eligible family member but the firstborn sitting across the table.

"Bill can't go."

Bill Bengston was Marie's husband, a quarter-blood who farmed his own place just off the reservation. Wife, kids, gimpy leg.

"Sophie won't let Lou."

Lou Monier was a good man, officially listed on the tribal roll, but Sophie bossed him.

"Leaves Pete."

"Uncle, you know Nora's due any day."

"Pete's too young anyway, got no sense."

"Who has?"

"Me."

Badger looked at the bag of old bones that was once the tribal runner of renown. During the summer hunt of 1859, a Brulé war party surprised the tribe, killed fifteen warriors and kidnapped three girls before the swift runner, nineteen years old in his bursting prime, raced across the front of their reforming charge, patted his bare butt in a rank, insulting challenge, and tolled them south into the rough country, playing bird with hurt wing, jumping rabbit, low-to-the-ground coyote, dodging, doubling, outrunning the Brulé war horses through the dying shank of day, coming at dusk to a deep, straight-sided canyon from which there was no escape, gave them a final insulting pat and went over. He woke in cold dawn with both knees swollen three times normal size; eight days later tribal scouts found him crawling over the prairie toward the river. They carried him home, nursed him tenderly, held a solemn ceremony in which his name was changed to Bad Knees, not in jest but to forever remind the tribe of his selfless courage. He had saved his people, and what had it gained him?

At twenty he became two men. The cripple boiled red cedar-leaf poultices, hunched over vapor baths of cedar twigs and coneflowers; traveled west to the stinking sulphur lake that never froze and squatted neck-deep in the steamy water; wet the ends of shoe-string weed, stuck the stems to his knees, burned them down to the skin; tried oils, fats, salves, sleeping under buffalo robes with both knees in a fat woman's belly. While the cripple hobbled about his useless cures, the inner man taught himself to think. He hated the Brulé Sioux for their strong bodies and handsome faces, the way they pushed out their big chins and walked the earth as sole owners. His first magnanimous act was widening his circle of hatred to embrace not only the Brulé, but all the boastful, arrogant, domineering Oglala, Sans Arc, Miniconjou, Hunkpapa, Blackfoot, and Two Kettle Sioux. He learned everything about them, at the same time watching white men until he too could win by cheating. Through eight years of intense raiding on the tribe by the Brulé, he became the master at setting ambushes in unexpected places. The Sioux named him the Limper, and white men called him by that name: Hoostay! Cripple and inner man became Uncle Bad Knees as he was in Badger's youth, as he still was, enigma to red, white, and brown, face fracturing like ice-split rock into what passed for his smile, puckered lips speaking words sweet as the black walnut-honey mixture he so dearly loved—words dipped in poison.

"Are you getting fat, nephew?"

"Got to eat to keep up my strength."

"Your strength rolls over your belt."

"I wear a tight belt, Uncle."

"Maybe you should try overalls."

Badger glared, saw his uncle open the peyote bag, went to the stove and put the kettle on. The tribe's

southern band had passed the peyote along to the
northern band a few years ago, and Uncle Bad Knees
discovered that peyote, eaten or brewed in tea, was
the only remedy that eased his pain. Friends in the
south saw that he had a constant supply for his bad
nights; as tonight, fingers counting twelve buttons into the boiling kettle Badger swung from the stove,
clapping the lid on, shoving the tapered corncob up
the spout. The tea steeped, Four-eyes whined softly
beside Badger's chair. He filled the cups, drank with
his uncle, rubbed Four-eyes behind the ears and felt
her rough tongue kiss his hand.

"A fine dog, nephew."

"Best we ever had."

"Your mother never looked at second-best. Laughed
at all the young men before your father came."

Talking to be talking? Never. His uncle evoked the
past to abate Badger's fear of violence born on the
day his father was murdered. Uncle Bad Knees told
his sister that all children feared their own shadows
at one time or another, it was part of growing up.
Badger the child overheard his uncle and envied
those other children. He was afraid of life's shadow
before he took his first kick at its substance. No wonder his uncle gulped tea and recollected how Badger's father had courted his mother in formal style
and married her twice, Indian and church, to show he
was not putting on a winter overcoat.

"That was a terrible year, nephew."

1877, year of tribal removal to Indian Territory.
Badger's father took his bride upriver to his brother's
place on the east bank, a few miles below his father's,
where Badger was born in '78, strong and well-fed,
while far to the south sickness and starvation deci-
mated the tribe. Standing Bear's son died in '79 and
the chief started north with the body, to bury his son
on the chalk bluff above the Missouri. A fragment of
the tribe, less than two hundred, chose to accompany
him. Their flight led to arrest, detention, and the
famous Omaha court case in which the presiding

judge broke all precedent and declared that an Indian was a person within the meaning of the law. Public opinion ran so strongly for the chief that he was permitted to take dead son, and live people, home; where the vicious charade continued. The government had ceded their reservation to the Brulé Sioux; only a government bureau could make an error of such idiocy. To resecure their homeland, the tribe needed more signatures of tribal or part-tribal descent on the official roll than the number of members come north with the chief. Badger's father offered the solution; he and other white men related to the tribe signed the roll that qualified the tiny northern band as reservation size.

They moved onto his mother's allotted share of reservation land. His father built the house, farmed, his mother gave birth to his sisters and brother, all lived together in a condition whites called happiness. Badger's father went with Uncle Bad Knees on horse-trading and fur-buying trips, worked for the tribal agent, became the chief's trusted interpreter; in the first week of 1891 he took his oldest son with him to Cheyenne River Agency on official business; sitting outside the agency building, Badger saw his father shot and killed for no reason by a complete stranger, one of the frightened Sioux from Wounded Knee. The son of thirteen became man of the family, member of the eighth clan, Sons of White Men, whose one taboo was not touching mice. Three months after his father's murder, the agent called him in and asked if such a bright young man wanted to go down south to Haskell Institute. Badger had heard awful stories about the Indians who went to Carlisle School. He ran all the way home and hid for a week, caused his mother and uncle to hold a big council. Years later his mother told him that she had wanted to keep him home until he lost his fear, because he had been the apple of his father's eye, the firstborn son his father held high hopes for, and it seemed she should respect her dead husband's wishes. Uncle Bad Knees agreed it was good to stay away from Haskell, but bad to think of hiding her son from the world. His nephew was not a coward, seeing his father shot to death had turned him inside out, so they must do something now or her son would develop the canny knack of making the worst of a good bargain every time.

Uncle Bad Knees had traveled up and down the river for years; it was natural that his nephew join him. Nobody looked twice at the old man and the boy rolling along the trails in the I.D. wagon. Uncle Bad Knees had prowled every creek and river on both sides of the Missouri from the Swiftwater north to the Cannonball; in good weather the river roads became Badger's school. His uncle taught him Sioux and sign language, winter counts, how to break horses in shallow water, hunt, fish, spear turtles with a pitchfork, pick edible plants, use a knife, and shoot a gun. Badger remained an indifferent shot but his uncle was not dismayed; the mind was the deadliest weapon and his nephew had an excellent mind. Learn everything, was Uncle Bad Knees' order, nothing was too small to remember, it might save your life one day. His uncle was a member of the tribe's first clan, the Snakes, expert trackers and readers of sign. Badger practiced those vanishing arts until he surpassed his uncle; and during those years he saw the country of the Sioux change forever.

The government sold grazing leases to the big cattle companies, Matador and Turkey Track, Three V's and Three C's, Mill Irons, H A T, Sword and Dagger, and L7's, millions of acres along the Cheyenne, Moreau, Grand, and Cannonball, and the railroads built track west to the Missouri. Evarts was the biggest shipping point, a little town with the hair on, the cowboys called it, where the railroad ended and the cattle crossed the river on the pontoon bridge. Badger had never seen dipping vats until the day in Evarts he watched the steers swim through the hot nicotine solution that killed the ticks; in time he saw the other rowdy, hard-bitten river towns—LeBeau and Chamberlin and Pierre—and heard cowmen say things like give one of them Sioux bucks a shirt, pants, blanket, and a white man's hat and he's willing to let the white man handle his business, but not them half-breeds, they're too smart. He stopped at Cherry Creek subagency on Ration Day and saw the Indian police go into the corrals with their big revolvers and shoot the Texas steers through the heart from the side, watched the teams drag the carcasses off to the villages where the butchering began and the cooking and eating went on day and night until the meat was gone. His uncle said that once the Sioux started living in houses like whites, they would start dying of the white man's diseases, the TB, syphilis, measles, blindeye, but mixed-bloods were tougher, they would survive. Badger was soon old enough to understand what he saw happening to the handsome young Sioux women. Already heavy-faced and thickened, they had the gunpowder tattoo dot in the middle of their foreheads. His uncle did not need to explain how Sioux whores were marked; nor did his uncle ever teach hatred for the Sioux. That was a natural function of the body, absorbed like air and water. Badger saw the Sioux become a captive race. Remembering his father, he felt no compassion.

And still he clung to youth, often argued gleefully that, if he was man of the family, why should he hoe corn and carry wood, that was sisters' work. His mother agreed in principle but reminded him that no one in the tribe had been pure Indian in custom for years, even his uncle spoke American better than their own language, so how could they, living side by side with whites, keep on doing many things they had half-forgotten. Badger rebutted by asking how it was in those bygone days, a cunning trick (or so he thought) that seemed to lure his mother under the nearest shade tree where she retold such stories as why cattail fuzz was used to wipe babies and curved bows were fastened to the front of cradleboards. She taught him the other side of his uncle's world; until he felt youth die and looked at life through the cold, sardonic eyes of the man he had become.

"Boil more water, nephew."

Badger filled the kettle, watched it boil, saw the peyote buttons drop. The third cup of tea loosened his belly muscles and released his bitter grief. That was the way with his family, others yelled, moaned, sliced arms and sawed off fingers, but his family choked back emotion until each crawled off into his, or her, private cave in the black night of despair. His uncle's voice, sanctimonious as an Indian agent calling unexplained shortages an act of God, pushed words through his sorrow.

"—yes, that settles it."

"What?"

"There's nobody—got to go myself."

"You can't."

"Who says?"

"Me—never said I wasn't going."

Abandoned hopes and shriveled dreams given new life raced delicately across his uncle's face. What an actor!

"Nephew, you'll go?"

"You heard me."

"Scared?"

"Damn right!"

"Will you find them?"

"Uncle, I'll try."

"Good, start now."

"Tonight?"

"Hitch up, my mare too."

Badger ran to the barn, fumbled stiff leather and cold iron, backed the little mare into the shafts of the light wagon, led her to the cabin door, ran back and trotted the paints to his wagon. The cabin door opened, his uncle called:

"Go on, nephew. Four-eyes will keep me company."

Luck, when least expected. Badger urged the paints from the yard, let them pick their own way down the old trail off the oak bluff through the hills,

across the north pasture into the barn. He unhitched
and unharnessed, ran to the house, lit a kitchen lamp,
closed the doors, pulled the shades, set the lamp in
the northeast corner. How much time did he have?

In the old days when doors faced east and fires
were built in the center of earth lodges and tipis,
tribal caches were dug in reference to those center
firepits; first choice was to the south, if a second pit
was needed, it was dug to the west, a third to the
north. Their house was built of trimmed logs on a
stone foundation, with board floors and caulked walls
and window glass. When Badger started the whiskey
business he told his mother to pick the cache. She
chose the northeast corner of the kitchen as safest,
working only when the girls and Pete were gone, Badger fixed the floorboard, dug the shaft, hollowed out
the cache hole, and fitted the half-gallon cream can.
Only he and his mother knew about the secret cache
into which he fed double eagles for eight years until,
last month, both agreed that as soon as he got home
from Gregory, it was time to decide what to do with
the money: nearly two thousand dollars.

Badger lifted the floorboard, dug the earth from
the shaft, reached down. The can was gone! Lying
on his face, he cried soundlessly. What if he had discovered the loss before his uncle tricked him into following the killers? Would he have volunteered to go
because they had stolen the money or murdered his
mother? He was afraid to answer his own question;
but he would take vengeance if he had to trail them
through the keyholes of hell. He tamped the earth
back in the shaft, replaced the floorboard, heard his
uncle's wagon as he set the lamp on the table.

"Nephew!"

"Yes, Uncle?"

"Bring the lantern."

Four-eyes sniffing ahead, Uncle Bad Knees led
Badger across the corral to the gate opening into the
big west pasture. His canes rapped the gate post.

"They went out here, crossed the pasture, took the

draw south to the road, headed west. Wagon, team, two saddle horses. All shod. I found hair on the plum brush in the draw. A sorrel horse. I measured the wagon tracks, my string said five feet, two inches on the yardstick."

"Wide track wagon, Uncle."

"Yes, and I measured three-inch tires. When were you last scratched for pox?"

"Year ago."

"Fresh cases upriver—" his uncle turned and led the way back to the house "—you got money?"

"Plenty."

"Time to pack—" his uncle limped into the kitchen, blinked against the brighter lamplight. Four-eyes growled softly and Badger rubbed her ears. His uncle nodded. "Four-eyes still smells them. She will stay with me. You follow their trail, stop at Mike's, I'll send him word."

"Uncle, you think they'll split up?"

"That breed? Can't stand their own smell long."

"Then how—?"

"Find where they split. Pick one, go after him, make him tell where the others went."

"Make him?"

"Same way they made your mother talk."

"Uncle, what kind of men—?"

"Don't care. Find them, kill them, bring me your mother's necklace, then I'll know you done it—" all the past was in that challenge; before he could reply his uncle touched the picture frame on the wall "—if they had broke this, I would kill them myself."

Over the years eight photographs had been mounted inside the big picture frame: father, mother, uncle, sons and daughters. Badger's father looked out from the last photo taken of him, in September, 1890, on the agency steps, a short-legged, deep-chested man, curly black hair ruffed by wind, smiling like the voyageur he might have been, that's why his legs were so short, he told them once, the canoemen got squashed down in the north country. Laughing eyes, broad smile, dead seventeen years.

"That's you on Pete's wedding day, nephew. You nearly choked."

The firstborn stood in the kitchen doorway, hair slicked down, eyes squinting against the morning sun, jaw stiff as his uncle's knees above the unaccustomed hard collar, tie, and store suit. On his right in order of their age were three snapshots of his sisters: black hair, big eyes, proud noses, strong chins, wide mouths, tall, full-bosomed, straight-legged.

"What fine girls."

"No run-arounds in that bunch, Uncle."

"Who you think is strongest?"

"Marie."

"Not Sophie?"

"Could be if she stopped bossing Lou."

"His fault, he don't beat her—what you say for Amelie?"

"Too young yet to tell."

"Hah, there's little Pierre!"

Bigger than Badger, powerful body straining the seams of his wedding suit, taken the same morning as Badger's, Pete grinned out at the camera. Married to Will Buckles' daughter Nora, living on one of the Buckles' allotments, puppies still playing at the business of life. Badger clicked his teeth.

"Little Pierre? Get him mad, he'll trim your toe-nails for you."

"Let him get mad, nephew. You keep your temper."

"Like her?"

"Like her."

They looked at his uncle's sister, his mother, an unposed snapshot taken by Amelie at the corral, caught exactly as she had been and would always be to Badger, to all of them if they saw her as he did in the heart. Wearing one of her old elkskin dresses that October afternoon, brown arms on the top corral pole, standing on tiptoe to see something going on inside,

stretching muscular legs through ample hips and
bosom into strong neck holding big head proudly,
black hair parted in the middle and combed back
from her high forehead into a thick club tied with red
ribbon. Eyes bright, square teeth gleaming, wearing
her necklace of silver beads, each bead one inch long
and a half-inch thick, twenty-four beads to each
strand, ten strands holding the Mexican silver mount
that clasped the big Arizona garnet. Kodaked five
years ago when she was nearly fifty, mother of five,
grandmother of six, looking younger than most wom-
en ever were, what bloods ran in her, through her to
them? In the old days all the explorers, trappers,
traders, soldiers, priests, and European noblemen
came up the river and left a good many nine-month
calling cards. Whatever, it had not hurt her or her
children, had given her that crooked smile, that scalp-
hatchet temper and equally fierce kindness, made
her a faithful friend or deadly enemy. Understanding
the natural extension of her brother's hatred of the
Sioux in her son, and his fear of violence, she con-
doned his selling whiskey to the Sioux and did not
blame her brother, the uncle looking out at the world
from the snapshot on her left, caught in a rare un-
guarded moment: sitting in the sun on the south side
of the house, one of Marie's children under his right
arm, left hand pinning Sophie's baby to the blanket
spread on the bench, Four-eyes and the older children sitting back to the camera, looking up raptly, he
plainly enjoying himself as he related some monu-
mental tale of long ago, canes against the bench, forgotten, sunlight warming them all, shining on one in-
nocent moment out of time.

2

He was crazy, charmed like a bird by that old snake of an uncle, rectum so puckered with cold and misgivings he couldn't pass lime to save a tail feather. Badger got down and walked around the wagon, yanked the tarp ties, slapped his arms across his chest; off south was the Swiftwater, north beyond the bluffline the Missouri, he was ten miles up the road that mudballed through country so raw it took fools and Indians to survive. He was fool, Indian, and French. What did that make him?

"Triple-be-damned fool!"

Under the tarp was a cockeyed outfit—grub, gumdrops, bedroll, clothes bag, Bull Durham, jelly beans, ropes, hay, corn, oats, horseshoeing kit, tool chest, veterinary case, gallon jug of kerosene, twelve-gauge double-barrel, medicine chest, odd box—put together with loving malice for a black-haired, brown-eyed, round-faced, greasy-looking man of normal size wearing a dirty gray hat, purple flannel shirt, Boss-of-the-Road overalls, knee-length sheepskin coat, and clodhoppers that shook the wet earth in cadence with his white breath balls that floated on the breeze into the paints' moist gusts; tender pink sunlight dried his greasy look and changed him into someone else. An army surgeon once asked his Uncle Lionel who was the best actor he'd seen; and Lionel Badger, a melo-

15

drama-lover who had watched *Ben Hur* performed in Minneapolis with real horses on a stage treadmill, replied, "Red Cloud, then my nephew Henry, or mebbe I got them hind-end-to." Lionel was always careful to obfuscate his nephew's sorcery.

Badger had the chemistry of a lizard, the anolean color-coating to stripe himself into any rainbow. All his life he had been ignored by one blood or the other, depending where he stood at the moment, and he made this supposed weakness his surest strength. Where Indians told a white nothing, he learned all; whites told him what they knew because he changed shape to prove their prides and prejudices. Most mixed-bloods spoke French, Indian and American so badly that nobody understood them in any language. Badger spoke all languages clearly, was never hindered if he chose to follow a cold trail to the frozen end. Yes by god, even if the barn was stolen while the horses were in the pasture.

"Get along, you!"

The paints flushed grouse and prairie chicken from the roadside ditches, blackbirds wheeled and flocked above the marshes, leaves had flamed yellow and red, faded, started to fall. Why did ash leaves shrivel up the most, turn the darkest brown, hang on the longest? For the same reason people challenged this country that broke plows, sent weaklings to the state hospital, killed lonely women faster than bereaved husbands could answer the matrimonial ads. Why not, birds of a feather ended up in the same pillow. Like him, they were crazy in their own way, pushed and prodded by unseen forces. In 1902 the railroad built the branch line from Swiftwater out to Bonesteel in the Rosebud reservation district and established trade towns at regular intervals along the tracks; the first wave of wool-hats opened stores and sold life's necessities to more of their own kind who tried uncallused hands at farming. What a pedestrian bunch to squat in Indian country; all of them lumped were one white corpuscle in the bloody Brulé bucket.

Unseen forces! Usually political, always crooked as a dog's hind leg. The government suddenly threw open the Rosebud in 1904, made every prospective buyer register for an assignment of claims to be drawn by lot: 2,500 quarter sections at $4 an acre. 106,308 persons signed for the lottery. The unlucky winners had barely learned to get through a winter when the railroad extended the branch line to Dallas in 1907; in that same eventful year the west end of the Lower Brulé Reservation on the west side of the Missouri between Pierre and Chamberlin was opened up, and two railroads staged a hell-for-iron race to Rapid City. The C & NW brought its first train into Rapid City on August 7th, 1907; the Milwaukee got there three months later. In 1908 the government offered 6,000 more Rosebud quarter sections, mostly at $6 an acre, the less desirable remainder at $4.50 and $2.50. 114,769 persons signed for the second lottery, the railroad ran fifteen trains a day bringing the eager thousands to Gregory and Dallas. Badger used that carnival atmosphere to pull off his biggest sale. He delivered three wagonloads of whiskey to the rendezvous northwest of Dallas without a hitch; he could have driven a herd of centaurs ridden by naked dancing girls through the land-hungry mob and never raised a deacon's eyebrow. It was the easiest money he ever made; all it cost him was two thousand in gold and his mother.

He lost the wagon trail in the road traffic, had no chance at all to identify the saddle horses, having nothing to compare. He camped on Twin Calf Creek, slept in the wagon, made an early start; stopped to talk with a family stacking corn shocks, gave the father a big pinch of snoose, told the children, "Close your eyes, cup your hands," and poured jelly beans. Further along he saw a woman hurrying down her lane to intercept him, waving something white. He waited at her mailbox until she leaned against the wagon to catch her breath and handed up a letter.

"I missed the carrier, would you mail it in town, see, I got it stamped."

"Glad to, ma'am."

Under the shapeless hat her eyes were already sliding in and out of present time into some unknown whitewashed country of the lost. Thin dress hanging on sharp bones, workshoes heavier than his, those eyes. He gave her three years, hoped she was worth a decent stone. He mailed her letter, addressed to a woman in Sandusky, Ohio, in the depot box, turned into the livery barn, and slept in his wagon; aching bones woke him at five a.m., how long would he last? He brought coffee and two plates of hot breakfast from the café. His kindness melted the night man's grouch, words whistled through mouthfuls of eggs, sausage and cornbread, answering Badger's questions.

"Two in a wagon, two riders? Nope, but there was two riders last week."

"One on a steeldust?"

"Black, and a stocking-legged sorrel."

"Talk to them?"

"No chance, they hauled early. One big galoot, one runt."

"Go west?"

"S'pose so, no place else worth going to."

Badger drove west, talked with everybody agreeable, which meant the entire countryside, most of them so eager for news from the outer world that he could have spent two weeks traveling twenty miles and never cooked his own meals. Nobody had seen a wagon, but a coltish girl herding sheep remembered the riders.

"He had a crooked nose and a funny ear."

"Which one?"

"The big one."

"Funny ear?"

She told her dog to watch the sheep and came over to the fence. She had on a pair of carpenter's blue denim overalls six sizes too big, bottoms folded into a

man's gum boots. Her protection against the elements
was a boy's black duck coat over a blue jersey shirt,
and an old blue kersey cap with the satin lining worn
to slick-stringed remnants that fluttered in the wind
when she pulled the cap off and scratched a mop
of straw-colored hair.

"Like you crinkled it with a curling iron."

"Or got hit."

"Would that do it?"

"Sure would, and last longer than a curling iron."

She laughed, grabbed the top fence strand in her
mittens, and scissored over like a high-jumper. She
was about two years and an inch from climbing out of
the pumpkin and throwing her loop over a Prince
Charming, but the way she accepted his jelly beans
while she rubbed the paints' necks, she was ready to
kick the prince into the pumpkin and take off with
Badger if he spoke one word in tune. Her voice reminded him of the Boston butcher homesteading up
the White River who learned never to wash all-wool
underwear in a kettle of boiling water. It went in
man-sized, dried on the line fit for a ten-year-old.
She had the same brand of faith in some private god
Badger couldn't see. He poured her another handful
of jelly beans and she stared at him in wonder.

"You want something?"

"No."

"Why the candy?"

"Because you're nice."

"So are you—" she cocked her head "—mixed-
blood?"

"Yes."

"I can see the French, but I'm not up on the Indians out here yet."

"What are you?"

"Some English, some Irish, some Portugee."

"Near Boston?"

"Maine."

"How old are you?"

"Seventeen."

"That's legal age."

"For what?"

Badger said, "Herding sheep," and flicked his whip. The paints responded, he waved it goodby, and she yelled after him, "What do you want with old crinkle-ear?" and when he turned and called, "Going to kill him!" she stared open-mouthed, then started to laugh and shook her yellow head helplessly. The woman back down the road could learn something about survival from the girl. You had to laugh to keep from going crazy but a lot of them couldn't smile to save their sanity. An hour later he crossed the state line into reservation country where, short years ago, the only white men west of the river worked for the Indian department or were married into the tribes. Those men were nearly all descendants of the original French-Canadians who came down the river in the early nineteenth century with the North West Fur Company, took Indian wives, stayed on, sired big families, ran big herds, lived an ingrown life that refused to see what was charging inward from every compass point. His father and Uncle Lionel knew them all, were related to some, told his mother stories she repeated to him when he was old enough to travel with Uncle Bad Knees. Badger verified those old tales with his own eyes and ears. They had been kings out here on the grass west of the Missouri. They built manor houses and barns of hewn logs chinked with wet gumbo that dried like plaster. The ridgepole held the roof logs, two feet of gumbo was shoveled on top, and notched logs spiked to the wall logs along the edge of the gently sloping roofs kept the dirt from sliding off. Built in the tree-lined creek bottoms, the houses resisted all extremes; in summer everybody moved outside into the brush arbors. There wasn't a dug well or windmill west of the Missouri, everybody used running water and always boiled the coffee. Their world was a leaky paradise that collapsed under the avalanche of white men's cattle.

"Hup, Sunny—hup, Brook!"

The paints raced darkness at a leisurely walk, entered Fairview at sunset, crossed the railroad tracks, went around the depot up the alley that ran beside the coal sheds to the unloading dock behind the cream station. Badger stepped from wagon seat to dock, looked through the dirty office window; and there in his swivel chair, boots on the rolltop desk, bottle open, glass at elbow, mind at ease, sat Mike Waddell, dragoon moustache, red silk neck scarf, game leg, watery wind-in-the-eye look old cavalrymen got chasing dreams. His honorable discharge from the 1st U.S. Volunteer Cavalry was framed above the desk; it and Mike's hearty greeting welcomed all strangers. He shook hands, gave them a fast size-up, told them he'd patted the alligator's ass (this omitted if ladies were present), packed the elephant's trunk, hung his hat on the wildcat's whiskers, rode up San Juan Hill with Teddy, and what was their pleasure: butter, milk, cream, or claims?

Hard-working, God-fearing Christians recoiled from the drunken Roman, asked for the claims locater who got $25 for spotting a good place and $30 for throwing up a shack on the land. They had it on reliable authority he was the nonpareil. When Mike bowed modestly, "That's me, have a drink, which way from town you want to go?" they realized that postulation caught no converts in this heathen land. They never took the time to wonder who he was, what he had done, who called him friend?

On the day they buried Henry Badger's father in January 1891, Mike Waddell came with Uncle Lionel Badger and many other friends from upriver. Mike stayed with young Henry all day, through the ride to the chalk bluff, down the bluff in a driving snow that threatened to become a blizzard. Uncle Lionel's party had to leave for Swiftwater, to take the boat across the Missouri; saying goodby, Mike gave the boy some man-sized words: "You'll know worse

days, lad. Face them the way you faced today, you'll
live forever." The door closed behind him, Badger
turned to his mother. She said simply, "A good man,"
and he knew that Mike Waddell was the best. But—
"Why did he come, Mother?"
"He belongs."
"With us?"
"We are his people."
"Red hair?"
"Listen—"
Redheaded, fair-skinned, freckled, shaped like an
Irish stevedore, showing no mixed blood; his father,
an Irish adventurer, came upriver in 1840, left the
boat at Badger's Landing, went to work for Grandpa
Lucien Badger. Six years later he married old Rene
Labate's daughter, a breathtakingly beautiful girl, and
moved upriver to the big Labate place. Mike was
born in 1848. His father and mother were drowned
in the spring of 1855 when their steamboat hit a
submerged snag in the fast, narrow gut between the
mouth of Sioux River and Omaha Creek. The young
captain, Horatio Perriwinkle, saved eight-year-old
Mike and delivered him safely to his grandparents,
who raised him with affection and the boisterous help
of eleven uncles and aunts. Mike had a way with
languages, worked arithmetic problems in his head,
and spelled worse than a French king. By the time he
reached his sixteenth birthday, in 1864, the love of his
uncles and aunts had changed to envy larded with
fear. Old Labate told everybody that Mike had more
savvy at sixteen than all the Labate whelps hung together; in river language it meant that his own children were apt to be displaced by a grandson, and a
damned redheaded half-Irish tiger at that. Labate
knew better, told Uncle Bad Knees that Mike had a
bugle stuck up his butt, it was a wonder he had
stayed home sixteen years. Two months later Mike
sneaked down to Omaha, lied about his age, enlisted in the cavalry; rode through Georgia with Sher-

man and came home a sergeant, thus fooling Labate
the second time.

Mike ran the place for his grandfather until Labate
died in 1872; before the uncles and aunts could use
rifle, knife or strychnine, he vanished. He stopped to
say goodby to his good friends, Badger's uncle and
future father, paid a respectful call on the chief, and
left the river country. Nobody heard from him until,
eighteen years later in 1890, he reappeared as suddenly as he vanished. He saw Badger's father in
Swiftwater and spent the afternoon telling where he
had been and what he had done. In 1872 he had gone
to Boston, found his father's family, could not stomach
them any more than they suffered him, took ship to
Montreal, worked his way west to the Cree country
and lived with his grandmother's family until he spoke
their language and felt he knew something about her.
Then he packed on to Vancouver, took passage on a
coastal schooner to San Francisco, and worked his
way down the lovely California valleys to Los Ange-
les; the year was 1874 and the bugle was still giving
him gallstones.

He enlisted in the cavalry and was assigned to a
regiment in Arizona Territory. Mike was the trooper
regimental commanders dreamed of: Civil War experience, expert with horses, men and weapons, lin-
guist who seemed to pick up Apache overnight. Best
of all, he enjoyed his work. Mike participated in the
closing campaigns against the Apaches, went north
with Crook, thereafter could call off one place name
after another in the endless list climaxed on the
Greasy Grass in '76. Mike stayed on, served under
Miles and Crook again, until he could no longer swallow what was going on west of the Missouri. He took
his discharge and turned homeward; not to a house, a
piece of land, but a country in the mind: the river
country from Swiftwater north to the border. He
asked Badger's father to give his respects to Uncle
Bad Knees, promised to visit soon, meet the family, as

soon as he saw Uncle Lionel. He never saw Badger's father alive again.

He went upriver to Lionel's, had a grand reunion, stayed on to help, finally agreed to think seriously about the foreman's job. By then it was Christmas, then New Year's, then the terrible news from Cheyenne River Agency. Mike came to the funeral, met the children, and going upriver in the blizzard, accepted Lionel's offer. He could keep books, cook, do blacksmith work, carpenter better than anybody on the place, and practice animal medicine that local horse doctors had never heard of. Mike had a sure-fire cure for lockjaw tetanus, the kind that made a horse's jaw get solid after a long run. Mike had the horse thrown, put a board on its forehead, and gave the board a helluva lick with the blunt end of an ax or sledge. He never lost a case; and soon he was noted for his inexhaustible fund of abilities.

He worked for Lionel through the '90s, bought and sold livestock, grain, hay, furs, shared in many a quiet little coup with Uncle Bad Knees and the fast-growing Henry Badger; occasionally packed a warbag and took a trip to unwind, but was never gone longer than three weeks. He was in Omaha selling a load of horses to McCreary & Carey of the Union Stockyards when the Hearst papers declared war on Spain. Lionel received Mike's wire the next day: the check was in the mail but Mike, unable to resist one last call to the colors, had signed with the Rough Riders. He returned from Cuba with a game leg and no desire whatsoever to take up the white man's burden. He stopped at Badger's, rode the new branch line into the Rosebud, and foresaw the future. He finagled the manager's job at the Fairview cream station, the first town across the state line, and grabbed the claims locater job when nobody wanted it. He settled happily in Fairview, content at last to snail along, and be damned if the town didn't rare up and grow like a weed.

Schoolhouse, standpipe, churches, stores, town hall,

and a generation of cigar-chomping merchants who called themselves boosters and went around slapping backs, glad-handing everybody in range, telling the world what a great little burg Fairview was. The ravens roosted on Mike's head and turned it toward the new schoolmarm, an angel-faced spinster who wore featherbone corsets, taught Sunday school, and hated children. They met at the Christmas party in the Odd Fellows Hall. She was impressed by his place in the community, his red hair, the freckles that gave him the ghostly, erroneous halo of the small boy. He lived alone in one of the best bungalows in town; it plainly needed a woman's touch. Mike was a strong, virile man while she, age as indistinct as the horizon on a windy day, was willing to stop teaching, the better to serve a worthier lord and master. They were married the day after school let out in May 1905.

The far-traveled veteran of the famous Rough Riders could judge men in an hour; with women, he told Badger on the climactic day in May 1906, it took a little longer. Say two centuries. Augusta started out to remake him in the image kept folded in her dreams; perhaps not so much image as a nice clean well-cut Butterick pattern, fifteen cents and this lovely shape is all yours. Her idea of the ideal man was two baths weekly, all over, daily shave, weekly haircut, clean collars, ties, watch chain, gold collar buttons, no strong drink or tobacco, nightshirts, Wednesday evening prayer meeting, Sunday church, with restrained concatenating on Saturday nights, but never after midnight. Then too, before they were married, Mike had called her Gussie, and still did, knowing she hated the sound of the dreadful word. But she could bear those small transgressions.

Mike let her do the house over from cellar to lightning rods: fresh paint, wallpaper, rugs, Roman divan, gondola couch, automatic davenport, two Morris rockers, one-hundred-piece rose-wreath Haviland dinner set decorated with pink climbing roses, gold-plated parlor lamp in rose pink to match the china, with wild geese decorations and a five-inch fringe of translucent pink beads; a new dining room outfit with a crumb set and a doodad Augusta called a pickle caster, silver-plated with a *fleur de lis* pattern handle and tongs; a remodeled bathroom with Gem tub, bowl and water closet, and a thirty-gallon hot water tank coupled to a Peerless water heater. For the hired girls, a Superba washer on the back porch, with twin rinsing tubs and a copper boiler; for her own pleasure, a fine buggy with side curtains, silver-butted whip, and a hot water bottle sack.

Mike stopped smoking, shaved off his moustache, never touched liquor unless outward bound on a two-day claims locating trip. He honored her respect for the Sabbath by crossing the hall to the spare bedroom at eleven-thirty every Saturday night; on a Sunday morning in May 1906, one year after their marriage, someone knocked. Augusta was putting on her switch, puffs and hat for church, Mike was shaving. She went up the hall, opened the screen door, saw Badger and Uncle Bad Knees, and ran screaming into the bathroom, spitting pins and perdition.

"Get that dirty savage off my front porch!"

Mike turned, razor poised: "—huh?"

"—and that greasy half-breed too!"

Mike thumbed his suspenders, went to the front door, saw the dirty savage and the greasy half-breed, told them to wait for him at the cream station, marched past open-mouthed Augusta into the kitchen, cracked the Acme fireproof safe and dumped the contents of the japanned deed box onto the table.

"Gussie, pick your half."

She recognized the end. Not the beginning of the end; the end! But the means escaped her.

"Who was that?"

"A famous chief and his nephew."

"Them!"

"His name is Bad Knees. He is my old and dear friend. His nephew is Henry Badger—"

"I knew it! I knew his mother was a squaw!"

Mike Waddell had never hidden or denied his birthright, but long periods of time passed when he did not think of what he was. He was alive in a lively world, what else mattered? At the same time he shared Badger's cynical sense of humor; both expected the worst and usually found it. Several times in the past Mike had deliberately kept his ancestry to himself, to better enjoy belated reactions. This time was not belated. He was not sure, even now, if it had been a conscious deception, or a response to something he had decided he wanted and sensed he could not get if he combed his red hair too far back from his brown heart. Now he was paying for his capture of her world filled with purity and golden light.

"Gussie, my mother's mother was métis."

"What's that?"

"She was the child of a French-Canadian bourgeois of the North West Company, and a Cree chief's daughter. I'll kill anybody—man or woman—who says one word against their memory."

Augusta had cocked her tongue to say several—but he was a stranger who spoke in a soft, cold voice that dripped hellfire—and closed it on all. This tolerable country had treacherously dropped a raging nest of horrors on her Anglo-Saxon head. She was married to a —she refused to think the word.

"You never told me!"

"You never asked—what do you want?"

"My furniture and rugs."

"Take them."

"Will you ship them?"

"Glad to."

"What are these?"

"Bonds."

"I'll take them."

"Fine."

"Is this all the cash?"

Mike lied: "—if you don't want it, say so."

"I'll take it."

She also took the evening train east. Mike was in the cream station office with his true friends when the bell rang, the whistle blew, and the driver wheels spun. Badger refilled Mike's glass. Uncle Bad Knees stared benignly at a wall calendar. Mike drank a farewell toast. Uncle Bad Knees actually smiled.

"Did you beat her goodby, Mike?"

"Uncle, I never laid a finger on her. Afraid if I did, she might change her mind and stay."

"You are a wise man."

"Uncle, I'm a damn fool, but I'm learning."

Several weeks later Mike received the divorce papers from her lawyer. He shipped furniture, rugs, china, and doodads to the enclosed address, traded the frilly curtains and fancy buggy for a good bay horse and stout wagon. He burned his high collars, ties and silk socks; got out his old clothes, dusted off his campaign hat, let his moustache grow, ran the cream station, and located worthy claims for unworthy idiots. He took a bath when he felt like it, which was oftener than twice a week if Augusta had only asked, and threw her forgotten hairpins, puffs, and talcum down the privy hole. He smoked and drank in moderation, played poker on Saturday nights, resumed his visits to a widow lady in the next town whenever she mailed him a chocolate cake. One evening during the summer just passed, helping Badger move three wagonloads of whiskey from Otto Ott's barn north of Fairview to Eddie Malone's barn south of Gregory, Mike swore that the worst mistake of his foolish life was not having the sense of recognize that Lionel's middle daughter had cared for him. Think of it, him!

Badger opened the office door, Mike leaped to his feet and greeted him with a bear hug, swung him around and smiled at the sight of him, lost the smile in the reason for Badger's presence.

"God, Henry, I'll miss her—oh hell! What can I say?"

"Don't try, Mike. Got any news?"

"Bits and pieces."

"Same here."

"You hungry?"

"Tired."

"Then off you go, sleep in a bed."

Mike walked him out to the wagon, waved him up the alley that ended three blocks south in the Waddell backyard. Badger carried his clothes bag into the kitchen, crossed the hall to the spare room, had the strength to unlace and toe off his shoes before falling backward into bed. He heard nothing until Mike called:

"Rise and shine!"

"Morning already?"

"Six a.m. Don't bother to dress."

"Never got undressed."

Badger washed in the kitchen sink, brushed his teeth with salt, poured coffee and sat at the table; propped in a chair facing him was Mike's large-scale map of the region thumbtacked on a sheet of wallboard.

"How many, Henry?"

"Four, over easy—what are these x's?"

"That one south of here—" Mike cracked eggs, turned bacon, pulled a pan of browned bread from the oven "—is where Grandpa Donahue saw two riders passing west. One black horse, one sorrel."

"Stocking-legged sorrel. I found a barnman who saw both horses and men. One big man, one little one. East of here I met a girl who saw them. She told me the big man on the sorrel had a crooked nose and a tin ear. Sounds like an ex-fighter."

"Yellow-haired girl, talks funny?"

"That's her."

"Her name is Andaman Littlefield, a sea captain uncle named her after the islands in the Bay of Bengal. Mother's dead, father's a dentist, come out here to raise cattle, mostly he sat in a rocking chair reading books while his livestock evaporated. Now they got sheep, he comes into town twice a week, pulls teeth, once he gets you strapped in the barber chair he starts telling you what a wonderful place Cape Porpus, Maine, is. He's harmless, she does all the work. She's one helluva girl."

"That x south of Gregory where they split up?"

"Eddie Malone's boys were fishing in Ponca Creek, watched them ride up from the east, made out some of their talk. The runt rode into Gregory, kept on going north. The big man crossed the creek and took the Springdale road. Which one you want to follow?"

"The sorrel."

"Wise pick. He'll stop in Springdale, go south or west, either way he hits the main line, can catch a train, be hard to trace. How do you want to travel this lap?"

"Leave the team and wagon, ride a good horse."

"Got one saddled—" Mike served their plates "— eat up, take a bath, put on clean clothes, I'll have your dirty duds washed. One last tidbit: Malone's boys heard the runt call the tin ear Punch, and Punch called the runt Snapper."

3

Young Patrick O'Doul, the Butchertown light-heavy was a lean man with a muley jaw, china-blue eyes, and practically no hips. Veteran fight fans watched him closely as he began his climb toward fame, fortune, and scrambled brains. Patrick had courage, dynamite in both fists, and speed to burn; in prelim bouts he rushed from his corner and threw leather so fast his opponents were flattened before they could uncover his possible weakness. It took the tough old club fighters in the semi-windups to weather his early barrage, slip the counters to belly, ears and jaw, catch the first sign of eye wince. A pro named Battling Bronson ended Patrick's dream of the diamond belt one hot afternoon in the Colma ring. He turned Patrick inside, raised his head with a jab, came off his pivot foot and smashed a lovely hook to Patrick's delicate mandible. The fans groaned.

"One-punch O'Doul!"

Shortened to Punch, the moniker stuck long after he quit the ring with a fluted ear, thrice-broken nose, and all his senses intact. His mother's brother, Shaun Ryan, invited him to work on the Ryan truck farm north of Half Moon Bay, growing prize vegetables for the carriage trade, but Punch was too smart for that con. Catch him hoeing broccoli and Brussels sprouts? He offered his rare talents to the embarcadero saloon-keepers, but sailors and toughs soon learned that a

31

swift kick on the big bouncer's shins sent him into
hopping paroxysms of agony, at which time one fist,
sap, or chair leg dropped him in the sawdust. He
began hitting the bottle, lost his job, retreated to the
tenderloin district where evil companions cosseted
him as the fall guy in their clever schemes; but Punch
had a natural instinct that made him bolt and run
while the law grabbed the so-called clever companions. His welcome wore thin, his family disowned
him, time sent him lurching from one town to another,
dumping empty bottles and broken dreams. The
shards reflected sun, rain and mortality; then he met a
flea of a man named Snapper.

Punch was in his thirties, but guessing Snapper's
age was folly. How did you count the year rings
burned into that leathery face, estimate the horses his
bow legs had gripped, the reins fingered in his sur-
prisingly graceful hands. Snapper was born and
raised on a mule farm south of Boonville, Missouri,
rode his first donkey at sixteen months, and showed
true rapport for his father's mules from the very
start. People gave him more trouble. He stopped growing in the seventh grade while his classmates became
towering louts who made his life unbearable. On his
sixteenth birthday he hiked into Boonville and rode a
Katy freight train to St. Louis where he got a job moving livestock in a slaughterhouse; eventually he met
the owner of a three-horse stable making the Illinois
fair circuit. He shoveled, fed, groomed, walked hots,
finally broke his maiden on a spinster mare in a
claiming race at Peoria.

Snapper rode on to bigger stables, better mounts,
and larger purses, a natural-born jockey headed for
the top; eight years later he was licking bottom. He
could ride any horse but the wild bronco inside him;
his taste for larceny was so violent that he went
the full route with the poolroom crowd, pulling, dop-
ing, setting up ringers, fixing races in original ways,
until the Eye barred him from all tracks. Even the
outlaw courses and the Mexican border circuit gave

him the cold shoulder. The only safe place for a man
on the lam, wanted in nine states and the province
of Ontario, was the road. Snapper learned quickly—as
Punch could not—that once a bo hit those ties he
never stopped. Snapper was coming up from El Paso
when he met Punch in Raton, New Mexico. Snapper
kept a twelve-inch, lead-weighted leather quirt up his
right sleeve for jokers who cracked wise about his
size; but Punch wiggled his tin ear in tune to his battered grin and his broken nose thickened his tongue.

"Where you ridin', Jock?"

Snapper grinned, "Where you fighting, Champ?"

They squatted behind a stack of ties out of the cold
wind while the yard goat made up a northbound con-
sist; hopped a gondola full of some powdery white
mineral that turned them into a pair of Ringling clowns
by the time they rode over Raton Pass to Trinidad,
Colorado. They ducked into a jungle on Picketwire
Creek, cleaned up, boiled some java, and had a
snooze. Next day they pooled resources—eighty cents
—and lay around the fire getting better acquainted.
Punch needed a manager, Snapper needed a horse.
They slipped into Trinidad that night, rolled a drunk
for nine dollars, and caught the midnight drag to
Pueblo, Little Pittsburgh, found a quiet cantina and
took a bottle of tequila to the table under the counter
wire. Half an hour later Snapper knew that Punch
could not drink but, once started, could not stop, always started a fight, and always lost. During the fra-
cas Snapper got jammed into the cue rack, the law
waltzed them off to the slammer for ten days hard
on the county, but they ate, washed, and blew
town clean. Punch looked back and sneered.

"Can take the whole bunch."

"Take the Keeley, Punch."

"I'm no drunk."

"You never have time, you start fighting and end
up chewing cold steel. What you need is less booze
and more education."

"I can read 'n' write."

"Punch, you are going to study for your pee-h-dee in travel."

Snapper took him north through Denver, Greeley, and Cheyenne, conducting open-air and rattler classes on living in the uncharted buffer zone between the law and respectability: how to avoid cops, eat, sleep dry, find clothes, cover ground fast, and follow the sun. An icy Montana wind sent them scudding for the west coast, but they were whipsawed in the canyon town of Wallace, Idaho, where the railroad bulls and the local law offered Hobson's choice: winter work in the mines or head east. They rode the NP to the Twin Cities where Punch learned the coarse, cold-blooded art of winter survival. They mission-stiffed patiently through the angel food to get free soup and a flop; things got so tough in February that Snapper almost went on the gooseberry, but a blizzard hit, they picked up change shoveling snow, and were still breathing when the first bird sang.

"Where to, Snapper?"

"I got an idea."

"What?"

"Tell you if we get the jack to try."

"How much do we need?"

"Fifteen, twenty."

"Jesus, we'll never raise that!"

"Have faith, pack your bindle."

A week later, lying in the grass under the right-of-way fence on the GN branch to Sioux City, they saw the drag pass, brakie fighting a bo in an open rattler doorway; the train chopped, both men rolled from sight, a big case tumbled out. They ran down and cracked a treasure trove of winter clothing. Punch cursed, "In May!" but Snapper said, "Here's our summer stake," and they hauled the load three miles east through the woods to a road where Punch stood guard while Snapper hiked back to St. Paul and persuaded a fence to drive out in his Reo truck. He paid them twenty-five dollars cash, less their pick of two outfits, for the lot. They went on to Sioux City where Snapper traded the overcoats to a riverfront pawn-broker for three blankets and a pair of battered binoculars. That night they hopped a drag to Sioux Falls; next morning Punch looked out and groaned.

"Snapper, this is godawful country. What do we want here?"

"Come on—" Snapper led the way from the train yards, bought a ruled bond paper tablet and two pen-cils in a corner grocery, went on around town to the ridge above the backstretch of the racetrack where, focusing the binoculars, he prepared for the opening day of the meet.

"Snapper, what—?"

"The tablet's for charts, Punch. My own form charts. We're roosting up here every day of this meet. We get the morning paper with the lineups, I watch them run and keep my charts. Most of the nags run-ning down there will puff all summer on the county fair circuit. Small town tracks don't have the Pinker-ton Eye playing watch dog. Nobody knows me out here. We follow them all summer, hit every track, when I see a horse I rate, a jock up I like, at the horse's best distance against average horses, at good odds, we bet. We never bet favorites, only the horses I figure can win at good odds."

"How many can we win, Snapper?"

"Win one bet in three, we make money."

They watched every race of the Sioux Falls meet, moved after the little world of horsemen and horses to the next town on the summer hayseed circuit; at the first meet after Sioux Falls, seven days of racing, Snapper made three bets and won one, enough money to live a month. They were on their way; as they traveled through summer, a few other foot-free faces became familiar. Other people followed the horses for business and private reasons, among the crowd a round-bellied, bouncy man who drove a camp wagon and led a string of trading stock. His name was Trader Brown. He had a daughter two inches taller than Snapper who kept him sober, did the cooking, washing, watched the stock, spoke American, Sioux and two or three other languages in a high, tight voice that turned guttural whenever she got excited or mad. They never saw her in a dress; the odds were 2–5, Snapper said, that she didn't own one, 3–5 that if she did, she'd put it on backwards the first try. Jeans, work socks, tennis shoes, cotton shirts, and a floppy sailor cap that hid her hair and most of her weather-browned face. She never bothered them, they respected her small privacy. Punch remarked once that Brown was stuck with her, and Snapper laughed softly at some private joke. He spent a good many evenings at Brown's fire, talking races and horses, while Punch was ruminating through the limited delights of rural fleshpots. Suddenly, unexpectedly, summer was gone. They bet on the last race of the last day at the Yankton meet, shouldered their bindles, and headed south, spoiled after three months of regular board and room. Somebody called "Ho!" and they turned as the big bay team pulled the camp wagon alongside, Brown on the seat with his daughter, trading string behind. Snapper said, "Hi, Trader, hello, Kid," and she ducked her head like a mink, jumped down, and walked back yanking halters. Brown aimed his corncob stem at Snapper.

"Where you heading?"

"Open road."

"Get-away money?"

"So-so."

Punch wanted to brag about having more money than a hick whorehouse, but evidently Snapper intended to keep that fact secret.

"Use some easy scratch, Snapper?"

"How easy?"

"Shooting fish in a rain barrel, but it takes four."

"Shoot."

"Let's cross over and camp."

They crossed the Missouri and went upstream a mile into the trees. After supper Brown opened a map of the area and pointed out the river, the town of Swiftwater, the Indian reservation, and the chalk bluff burial ground of the tribe where, in two days' time, they would bury their old chief. Brown drew an x marking the exact location of a particular farm on the reservation, drew another x one mile west and two miles south of the farm. He tapped that x with the eraser.

"Day after tomorrow, at dawn, we meet there."

"Thanks for the cracker jack," Snapper said. "What's the box prize?"

Brown said: "All that day, every Indian in the tribe will be on that chalk bluff, burying their old chief. The other is the farm I been trying to get into for three years. Somebody was always home, and worst of all, you never knew where all them other Indians were."

"How many on the farm?"

"Mother, son, youngest daughter."

"But not day after tomorrow?"

"Mother and daughter on the chalk bluff, son's out around Gregory."

"What if it rains?"

"They bury him if there's a tornado."

"So what's your deal, Trader?"

"Fifty-fifty."

"And the prize?"

"Gold—thousands."

Snapper said, "I don't know much about Indians, but a rich one up here?"

"Whiskey."

"Come again?"

"The son sells whiskey to the Sioux."

"That's illegal."

"So's the money he makes. He's got no bank account anywhere I can find, so he must keep it at home."

"Thousands?"

"He's been at it ten years, Snapper. What do you say?"

"Punch?"

"I'm with you, Snapper."

"We're in, Trader. But how do we get out there?"

"I loan you horses, you leave tonight, make a big swing south, we follow behind."

They rode wide of Swiftwater and hit the crossroads at dawn on the second day. Punch had to look twice before he recognized the camp wagon minus white duck top and bows. Brown led them the two miles north and one east, swung up a tree-lined lane into the farmyard, jumped down and inspected the yard while his daughter drove behind the barn. They tied the horses to the wagon and went into the house; hours later they had nothing to show but a handful of silver dollars.

"Trader, we missed it."

"Where, Snapper?"

"Let's go back—start at the top."

Brown's daughter called from the bedroom: "Nothing up there."

"All right," Brown said. "Cupboards?"

"In the walls?"

"Could be."

They were so intent that the squaw caught them off guard. Home long before she was expected, she leaped soundlessly from her wagon, grabbed the ax off the chopping block, and came through the kitchen door with a yell. Punch was standing on a chair, prying off the backboard of a cupboard shelf, Brown and his daughter were on hands and knees, testing the floor under the stove, Snapper was sitting at the table, making sketches of each room. She missed decapitating him only because he was small and agile, spun under and dove away from her flat swing; she recovered without losing stride, bounded around the table, necklace swinging at her throat, and let drive at Brown. His daughter rolled away from the stove

and threw the poker into her legs, knocked her off
her feet as Punch dived from his chair and got a
shoulder into her side; even then she bounced upright and brought the ax halfway through a vicious
swipe at Punch's neck before Brown deflected the
blade with his pinch bar. The clanging shock of steel
on steel made her drop the ax. Brown's daughter
caught the handle and jerked it away from her lunge,
Punch landed on her back, grabbed her arms, forced
them behind her while kneeing her down on her face.
Brown yelled, "Chair!" and Snapper whirled with
one. "Put her in it!" and Punch boosted her up, sat
her, arms behind the chair back. Brown tied her
crossed wrists with wire, slammed her legs against
the front chair legs, and wired them.

"Now, you red bitch, where's the gold?"

She spat in his face. Brown gave her an open-
handed clout that tumbled her against the wall. She
lay on her side, feet bottoms turned awkwardly up
by the wire.

"Set her up, we ain't got all night!"

Punch lifted her, and the chair, into place. Snapper
led him outside, both saw a quick flash of movement
at the barn corner.

"What was that, Snapper?"

"Dog—listen, take a look at her wagon."

Punch searched the wagon from tongue to tailgate.
Snapper went back inside, appeared again in the doorway.

"Any luck?"

"Nothing."

"Can you put that rig in the barn?"

"Sure."

Punch drove the squaw's wagon inside the barn,
closed the front door, unhitched and unharnessed the
team, left the back door open so they could go into
the corral, climbed over the fence, and ran to the
house. He got one look inside, then Snapper hustled
him back to their wagon, told him to ride ahead
and open the gates into the west pasture. Brown and

his daughter came running, all followed Punch across
the big pasture into a draw where Brown took the
lead. Riding behind the wagon, Punch said:

"Snapper, she was dead."

"She saw us."

"You never said anything about killing—"

"Punch, she saw us. If we got pinched, she'd nail
us to the cross."

"That's right."

"No other way, Punch."

Brown led them to the road, turned west and drove
as fast as the bay team could pull the wagon; ten
miles beyond the reservation he swung into a cottonwood grove, jumped down, and kicked the brush off
canvas and wood. They helped seat the bows and
pull the white duck cover up and over, tie it in place.
Brown's daughter returned from deep in the woods
with the trade string, tied them behind the wagon,
and jumped up beside her father. Brown said, "Giddap!" and they kept going that night and next day,
camped the following night in a ravine not far from
the Missouri. Brown wrote bills-of-sale for the sorrel
and the black, so nobody could accuse them of horse-
stealing. Punch slept beside the fire, woke shiver-
ing when Snapper passed the coffeepot under his nose.

"Drink up."

"Where—?"

"On their way."

"Why?"

Snapper patiently reminded Punch that the law
was looking for a wagon, team, two saddle horses, and
four people "—if anybody can read tracks, which
Brown doubts, besides, it rained last night. But one
man and his girl in a camp wagon with a string of old
plugs? He says a good many people know them, and
they don't add up to four. And us, two gents traveling
peaceful, do we look dangerous? Not on your tintype.
Besides, the law don't get excited over dead Indians."

"Who says?"

"Brown."

"How does he know?"

"This is his country, Punch."

"Snapper, the way you're talking, we're about to split up."

"Stop fretting. We'll amble along, be civil to everybody, once we get far enough west, we'll talk about splitting."

"For good?"

"No, you bonehead! We'll fix it to meet up again."

"Where?"

"At the right time. Now, listen close. I'm going to tell you what to say if somebody asks what you're doing."

Snapper drilled the story into Punch while they rode west. They spoke to a few hicks, stopped overnight in one town, slept in the livery barn, got away early; by the time they reached the big creek south of Gregory, Punch could reel off his sob story without a mistake. It was time to split. Snapper made him memorize where he was going, how to get there, where they would meet one month from this day.

"Got it clear?"

"I got it, Snapper."

"So long, Punch. See you in the funny papers."

Punch watched him ride north, turned the sorrel south across the big creek, made the long, lonesome ride to Springdale, a wide spot in a dusty road. He paid the barnman fifty cents, with permission to sleep in the hayloft, but no smoking. Punch said, "Nosirree!" and headed for the café, saw the saloon, took one step, and heard Snapper's voice. "Better run sober than die drunk on a rope." He retracted his step, went on to the café, ate supper and went straight back to the feed barn. He made his bed in the hayloft facing the open west door, tried to sleep, tossed and pitched, started holding his Ingersoll up to the starlight every ten minutes, finally packed and rode to the forks. On south was a town named Ainsworth that, according to Snapper, had a tough town marshal. Punch knew those bastards thought nothing of taking an unwanted man down the tracks five or six miles and telling him to hit the ties and never come back. Better go west, Snapper suggested, out in the sandhill country on the Swiftwater was a town named Ophelia.

Mike led a long-barreled chestnut horse from the barn and handed the reins to Badger.

"Meet Ashcan."

"Looks like a night-eye."

"Regular old tomcat in the dark."

"Circle horse?"

"Bought him off a Sword and Dagger cowboy, told me he could go all night, never break down."

That was the job circle horses were picked to do: run those long miles around a grazing herd, keep it up all night, never too fast or slow, just nice and steady. Badger tested the cinch, tied his gear on, mounted, fiddled with his hat brim, his coat buttons, gave Mike one last look. No hope. He said, "Get along, Ashcan," and Mike watched man and horse out of sight before turning to the barn.

"*Très bien*, Louie!"

Louie Allard came from the harness room, stroking his short black beard. Louis smiled like old Saint Nick, no matter he was giving candy to a niece or sticking his knife in a *cochón*. Uncle Bad Knees had sent Louie in person to help Mike.

"Tink he's mad?"

"Louie, he's cussing us from hell to Broken Bow."

Five miles down the road, sunrise shone on the lizard sporting his latest skin: gray Stetson, gray flannel shirt, black serge pants, flat-heeled boots for riding and walking, canvas-backed windbreaker, slicker tied behind. The chestnut moved in a mile-eating lope over the black ribbon unreeling across the brown prairie under the washed blue sky; sixty miles to Springdale, long day for a good horse, crotch-splitter for a good rider. The sun passed zenith, wind blew cold over the grassland never meant to be chopped

up and fed to a plow; thunderheads piled above the
Missouri, distant rumble twitched the chestnut's
ears. Lightning killed too many people out here, the
idiots crouched under trees or stood in water—or
rode in the open! This country needed water, in the
growing months it was usually dry as a wire corn
popper, full of hot winds, dust, and grasshoppers.
Lightning sizzled, the town lights jumped suddenly
from darkness, electricity charged the air as the
chestnut blew into the feed barn on the wind. The
barnman wrestled the big doors shut, dropped the
bar, and swung one arm at the empty stalls.

"Take your pick."

"All by my lonesome—" Badger unsaddled, led the
chestnut to a center stall; while he hung saddle
and shook pads, began brushing the damp coat, wind
died and hail beat a rousing tattoo on the roof "—business always this slow?"

"Hell no! Last week I had me an overnighter."

"Lost?"

"Could be, big mutt on a stocking-legged sorrel,
asked the best road to Ophelia, bedded in the loft,
damned if he wasn't up and gone at three a.m."

Badger ate the cold supper Mike had packed, slept
through the storm, woke at two and smelled dry wind
under clear sky, packed and rode at two-thirty. If
Punch had played it cute, asked about Ophelia and
headed for Ainsworth, Badger could save time riding
straight to Ainsworth; then, if Punch had gone to
Ophelia, Badger could catch a fast mainline train to
Ophelia and still save time. How much? Depended
where Punch was tonight.

4

Ophelia had a silver cornet band that sounded like
the pure cries of happy angels. The band led parades,
played concerts, and spearheaded special events; on
the afternoon Punch rode into town it was marching
back and forth on the baseball field, playing spirited
marches while executing intricate maneuvers. Punch
reined over beside the third-base bleachers and
watched a flawless rightabouttotheleftHUP—bythe
rightflankHUP—rightfaceHUP—inplaceHALT. Punch
applauded vigorously. The bandmaster saluted,
the bass drum player waved his buckskin head
stick, they were off again, bass on the major beat
bumBUMbumBUMbumBUM, snares tickling the
minor leftleftleft while the bandsmen took the silent
signal and satirized the old army cadence-count in
perfect time "leftleftleftleftmywifeandthirteenkids"
and the bandmaster raised his baton "SoundOFF!"
and the bandsmen responded "HUDDUPTHRUP-
FRUP!" as they marched away from the sunset.
Punch loved bands playing Sousa marches, his sweet-
est memories were pastiches of parades that formed
in front of the old Ferry Building and came up Market
Street in a blaze of sound and color; bands, drum and
bugle corps, flags, floats, bunting, cops, cavalry, in-
fantry, artillery, marines, sailors, coast guard, veterans, presidents, generals, opera singers, baseball players, heavyweight champions, governors—riding

44

through life the way it ought to be twenty-four hours
a day every day of the year, in a time when he still
smiled from the heart.

"You like 'em too?"

Punch looked up at a sandy-haired man sitting
on the top bleacher plank, grease-pitted hands holding a lunchpail and cap on his knees. He had a good
smile. Punch returned it.

"Sure do. What they practicing for?"

"Firemen's Day."

"When's that?"

"Fourteenth, next Wednesday."

"Parade?"

"Big one, and contests—"

"Tug-of-war?"

"Twenty to a team."

Punch grinned. "Over a pit?"

"Full of mud! Stick around, glad to have you."

The sandy-haired man put on the soft-billed cap
and came down the planks to the gate. His shoulders
were as wide as Punch's and twice as thick. Punch
warmed to him.

"Say, there a clean, cheap hotel in this burg?"

"Down on Railroad Street, I ain't promising you
it's the Ritz, but you need a barn too, and there's one
just a block off."

"You going that way?"

"To work."

"Swing up—" Punch gave him a forearm, he levered
himself lightly behind the cantle "—which way?"

"Any of these avenues south."

"You're a railroader."

"Shops."

They rode south to Railroad Street, west along the
tracks to the depot. The sandy-haired man slid off
and pointed west. "Thanks, there's the hotel, barn's
on down."

"Can I buy you a beer?"

"No time, I'm on the six to six, but see you tomorrow
around five in the saloon behind you."

He joined the stream of men flowing over the tracks into the shop area. Punch rode past the Rosebud Hotel to the livery barn, paid three days in advance, carried his bedroll to the hotel and signed for a room on the second floor rear next door to the bathroom, dollar a day seemed steep but that might be the celebration. He washed face and hands, found the nearest café, ate supper for thirty-five cents; it was dark when he crossed the street to the depot and read the train board in the waiting room. The passenger west at 2:15 a.m. and the passenger east at 4:30 a.m. were the best getaway times if he wanted to buy a ticket and ride the cushions. On his way back to the hotel he stopped at a cigar store, bought the *Gazette* and three big red Washington State apples, passed a good-looking skirt in the middle of the block and wished he could stay for the celebration; lying in bed, reading about Tommy Burns' last fight in Melbourne, Australia, and eating apples, he thought why not? and fell asleep smiling at the sagging, stained wallpaper with the core in his hand, did not wake until the shop whistle blew at six a.m. He dozed until eight, shaved in the wavy mirror, went next door for a bath, dried himself on the hotel towel that was made from somebody's shirttail after the shirt was thrown away. He ate breakfast in the same café, then strolled along Railroad until he saw a blue Australian wool sweater with ribbed neck and cuffs in a gents' clothing window. He bought it, a pair of black corduroy pants and a sheepskin-lined corduroy coat, three flannel shirts, two suits of underwear, socks, blue bandannas, ankle-high boots soft as carpet slippers, and an octagonal crown cap of dark cassimere suiting that fitted tight. He carried the bundles to the barbershop where a short haircut made the cap a perfect fit; back in his room he changed from the skin out, wrapped his old clothes in the bundle paper, and pitched the bundle into the dustbin. Feeling frisky as a kid, Punch walked north toward the main business district, legs in better shape than he could remember,

Snapper had said that getting in good physical condition was an extra dividend from their summer's work. Punch passed the big, fancy hotel, larger stores, counted six automobiles, paused outside a drugstore and watched the carpenters across the street put finishing touches on the World Series scoreboard bolted to the brick wall of the newspaper building; a scaffold was rigged outside the windows so the telegrapher inside could take the game off the strings and call it to the reporters on the scaffold who moved the wooden dowel sticks around the infield and called each play through a megaphone. By the time he returned from walking east to the ball park, north and west to the fairgrounds, and south to Swiftwater Street, a crowd had gathered for the opening game. Punch ducked into the drugstore, bought a sack of peanut brittle, and stood on the cement block under the west edge of the green-and-white-striped awning; two hours and another sack of peanut brittle later, the Cubs had won a loosely played opener 10–6, Brown the winning pitcher, Summers the loser. Punch walked south on Pine Avenue, waited on the corner of Railroad and Pine until the sandy-haired man joined him, wearing a clean shirt, clean overalls, whoever was chief cook and bottle washer in his house was a good one. They stepped into the saloon, took the front corner of the bar, and Punch said:

"Name your poison."

"One beer's my limit before work."

"You mind if I drink ginger beer?"

"Lord no, don't drink much myself."

Punch ordered and turned, foot on the rail: "My name's Pat O'Doul."

"Ossie Dressler."

They shook hands, lifted their drinks, smiled. Punch said, "You been here long?"

"Six years, come out from Cedar Rapids. My sister's husband got killed and she wasn't getting over it, so I got a transfer and brought her along."

"Make her feel better?"

"Whole lot, say, where you from?"

"Frisco."

"What the hell you doing here?"

Punch told the story Snapper had made him memorize: how his kid sister had run off with a bastard the family never knew about, that was two years ago, right after the earthquake and fire, and not a word until last May. She wrote for help, she was in Dakota, but she forgot to say where and the postmark was smeared. So he had come back to Sioux Falls and talked to the cops and they said buy a horse and work west. He had, hadn't found a smell, winter was coming, he was ready to quit.

"You think he left her, Pat?"

"Likely."

"I'd like to be there when you find him!"

"Nothing to see."

"Come on, Pat!"

"Ossie, I'm retired, but I can still get sent up if somebody swore out a complaint."

"For what?"

Punch made two big fists: "On account a pug's fists are called weapons, see, outside the ring."

Ossie nodded. "I figured you'd done some fighting."

"Ear and nose are dead giveaways. I ain't sensitive. I was smart enough to quit with my brains still working. One tin ear and a busted beak is a cheap price. Besides, I don't believe in fighting outside the ring."

"Say listen, Pat, why don't you come over tomorrow for breakfast with me and Sis. I get up at one if you can eat then."

"Sure your sister won't mind?"

"Be good for her. She still worries me. Six years and god knows Herman was a good man, but dead is dead, and she ain't looked at nobody since. Part of that was coming out here, it took time to get acquainted, but now she acts like she's happy keeping house for me. What the hell am I complaining for, she's a fine cook and you can eat off the floor, no kidding."

"Don't worry, Ossie, she'll meet a good man one of these days."

"Hope you're right—well, time to go."

"Hey, where do you live?"

"Up Pine two blocks, yellow house on the southwest corner of Pine and Sandhill."

The minute Ossie's sister opened her front door, Punch knew he had to be careful. Stepping into her house was being carried back to his boyhood when his Ma boxed his ears for tracking mud and knocking over the Virgin. Elvira wouldn't be interested in anybody as rough as he was, so he could be himself and stop worrying about putting on airs. He followed her into the kitchen where Ossie was adjusting the damper behind the stove. They shook hands, sat at the table, and Elvira asked:

"Mr. O'Doul, eggs or pancakes?"

Punch turned red.

"Ossie, did I say something wrong?"

Punch grinned. "First time anybody's called me Mister since I shook hands with Corbett."

"James J.?"

"He was the new champ, Ossie. I was just starting, he came by the gym, my manager introduced me. He called me Mister and wished me luck."

"Mr. O'Doul—?"

"Ma'am, please call me Pat."

"Pat, eggs or pancakes?"

"Eggs, ma'am."

"Pat, please call me Elvira."

They all started to laugh. Elvira had been sober as a judge, pretending she didn't know who James J. Corbett was, but Punch saw that she hung that look of shy dumbness on any handy collar button. She knew what she was doing all the time. Ossie was right, she kept her house neat as a pin, enjoyed cooking, living an orderly life with her brother who, Punch saw now, was in no rush to get married and throw away treasure for some bit of fluff. She was a year or two older than Ossie, which accounted for the occasional motherly touch in her eyes and words, and made Punch better understand why Ossie worried about an older, widowed sister.

"—shame about your sister, Pat."

"Huh—oh, excuse me, Elvira."

"You don't hold much hope this year?"

"Not now."

"What will you do?"

"I don't know."

Ossie said, "You got a regular job in Frisco?"

"No."

"Then why go all the way back this winter, if you figure on looking again next summer? Why not stay here?"

Elvira blushed, a delicate pink around the lobes of her ears. Punch looked steadily at his coffeecup: "Ossie, I'm no railroad man, and it looks like this town's strictly railroad."

"Looks fool, Pat. This is cattle and hay country, railroad's only the servant of the people—"

"Poppycock!" Elvira said. "That's what the railroad wants us to think. Look at you, best machinist in the shops, only man who can run that wheel lathe right. Why don't they make you foreman in the locomotive shop? You're the best man. Pat, take a tour with Ossie this afternoon, see for yourself if you'd like to work in the shops."

Ossie had been right about her dead husband, she was warning Punch away from a railroad job. He sipped coffee, wondered what killed her husband, watched them argue, an easy sparring match between old friends who relished the action but didn't want to score points. It gave him a chance to study Elvira closer. She had silky brown hair, darker colored than Ossie's, parted in the middle and wound into two braid wheels. She had on a blue and white gingham house dress that made him think of flowers; walking to the front door with them, he realized that she stood nearly level with Ossie, who was not a little man. She was wearing low-heeled shoes, too, and she wasn't as thin as he thought on first look. He meant it when he said:

"Elvira, that's the best breakfast I've had in years."

"Then you better hope supper's as good."

"I can't—"

"Ossie says you can—" and she was gone inside with a flick of her fingers across his coat and that shy, leaping smile. Ossie said, "Women!" and led him south across Railroad through the depot where they read the score of the second series game on the bulletin board: Cubs 6, Tigers 1; winning pitcher Overall, losing pitcher Donovan. They walked across the tracks into the shop area, quiet and almost deserted on Sunday. Ossie took him inside the steam locomotive shop where Ossie's baby sat, a huge piece of machinery called a wheel lathe, used to turn driving wheels and journals down; in simple language it meant making the wheels exactly round again, with no burrs, after a long, pounding session on the rails. Ossie said, "She's easy to run," and made Punch remember an old trainer who told him that the easiest punch a good fighter delivered was the one that came from ten years of long, hard practice. Ossie's lathe was about as simple as that to use correctly.

"This way, Pat."

Punch had figured himself something of an authority on railroads. He knew engines, cars, tracks, ties, rails, signals, lights, switches, conductors, brakemen, bulls, and depot agents; but he had not been inside the shops where men kept the moving metal of that system in running order. Ossie guided him through the maze in the same way a locomotive would enter in need of repair, overhaul, even a new part. It went first to the erecting shop where it was taken completely apart and those parts trundled off to separate section bays set up to do specific jobs. After which, all the parts were trundled back to the erecting shop and reassembled into the original locomotive. All locomotives needed regular inspection, greasing, and oiling after a run; once a month the boiler must be washed inside to clean out the scale. The locomotive edged along one of the approach tracks onto the turntable, which revolved until the locomotive eased onto the tracks leading into the proper roundhouse bay. A man on the catwalk lowered the smokejack over the smokestack, to draw off engine smoke while the crews worked. Ossie said, "That's enough for one day," and they retired to the saloon for beer and pretzels.

"How'd it hit you, Pat?"

"Man's got to be good to work there—" Punch did not add that, the way things looked, a man had to be crazy. He wondered how many were killed and injured every year.

"You could learn, Pat."

"Not me, Ossie. I'm all thumbs."

"Stay for the celebration, look around meantime, I'll see what else might be open."

"Don't you go to a lot of trouble, Ossie."

"It's a pleasure, Pat."

They went home, played checkers until Elvira called them to supper; on Sunday nights she and Ossie had cold cuts, potato salad, and rye bread, each made his/her own sandwiches and made fun of the other's. After that, because Ossie did not go to work until Monday at six p.m., they often took a walk uptown and window-shopped. Punch walked with them, found himself nodding when they spoke to other people, and when they got back he asked if they had lived in the house from the start. Ossie told how he had come out to scout the town, dug up five houses for sale, Elvira picked this one when she arrived. They moved in two weeks later, had been here ever since. Elvira smiled and patted Ossie's arm.

"He makes it sound easy, Pat. It wasn't."

Ossie winked. "Who do you think did all this inside work?"

"Not you."

"Ha, nosir, not me! Sis picked the wallpaper, found a sober paperhanger, then she painted the tricky spots and laid the carpets—"

"Pat, who do you think changed all the bathroom fixtures, replaced the window sash, patched the roof, rebuilt the cellar steps, painted the outside—"

"Yellow's your favorite color."

"Yes."

Ossie said. "How long did it take us, Sis?"

"Just over a year."

Elvira poured coffee and cut pound cake. Somehow or other, Ossie remarked that anything worthwhile took time and work, he was willing to bet the fight game was no different, and Punch found himself talking about his own experience for the first time. He had never thought about the way it was in the beginning, all boys had their starts, but there was a sameness running through the fight game, a common thread of entwined triumph/agony that held them together.

"How did you start, Pat?"

"Eleven prelims in a row, seven by KO."

"What's a KO, Pat?"

"Knockout, Elvira. I could hit good."

"Then what?"

The papers gave him a few lines, he fought ten more bouts with youngsters his own age, the survivors of at least a thousand hopefuls up and down the coast, as far inland as Salt Lake, Butte, Spokane. He won those bouts—

"That's twenty-one straight, Pat."

"Yes, Ossie—" my god, the impatience! He felt himself improving, wanted a shot at better fighters, but his manager was dead set against going too fast. He trained week after week, suddenly he was in the six and eight rounders, the fights before the semis, getting more money, but still going into the ring with his own generation and the relics from older generations on the downhill toboggan. Finally his manager signed with a tough old club fighter, eight rounds, that was a great moment for him. It was also his reckoning day.

"What happened, Pat?"

Punch touched his own jaw at the pivot, made a fist, threw a slow, soft punch across the table to Elvira's small chin, knuckles dusting her mandible point where the nerve lay. Her eyes widened in understanding.

"You got hit?"

"I got hit," Punch repeated. "Found out I had a glass jaw."

"It broke?"

"No, means I was an easy KO."

"What a shame!"

"I was overdue, just lucky nobody had tagged me before. Once they knew, it was Katy bar the door. I could handle the—" Punch started to say kidney "—body blows and head shots, but those old pros always broke through and I'd hear the birdies sing. I quit before I got hurt."

"I'm glad you did, Pat."

"Me too," Punch said. "I still like band music."

Ossie smiled. "You'll stay for the celebration?"

"Yes."

"That's great!"

On Monday afternoon Punch helped Ossie unload and stack kindling in the woodshed. Elvira came out and offered to bet five cents on the Tigers. Punch called her bet. That was the day the Tigers, two down, rose up and whipped the cubs 8–3; on Tuesday afternoon Punch bet Elvira another nickel, heard the final score in the café, went to the livery barn and told them to sell the sorrel. Ossie was waiting on the corner of Railroad and Pine when he got there.

"Sorry I'm late, Pat."

"I got held up too, Ossie."

"Listen, will you take Sis to the auditorium tonight, there's a town meeting."

"Glad to, if these clothes are all right?"

"Fine—" Ossie looked at the depot clock "—Sis says have supper with her at six, meeting starts at eight. So long, got to go!"

Ossie was wrong. The meeting started at four minutes past six. When Ossie headed for work, Punch ran back to the hotel, shaved, took a bath, put on clean underwear, shirt and socks, brushed his coat and pants, and knocked on the front door at five minutes of six. Elvira called, "Come in, Pat!" and he was hanging his coat and cap on the hall rack when the shop whistle blew the shift change. He said, "Elvira?" and she answered, "In here, Pat," but he hesitated because that was her bedroom. She called, "Pat?" and Punch went in. His last coherent look at anything was the ormolu clock on her dresser; it read four minutes past six when she finished undressing him and turned off the light. She was stronger than she looked, and once he got hold of her he knew why she wore her dresses loose. If the men in this town ever saw what she was hiding—a tiny voice in the back of his mind thanked the healthy summer he'd spent, otherwise he could not have survived the early fall. She turned on the light at 7:15, kissed him on the cheek, "I owe you a nickel, Pat. Hurry and get dressed, we can eat and still be there in time," and they were. Punch dozed in the tinder-dry heat from the hot air furnace, vaguely aware that Elvira's neighbors were discussing a site for something and arguing about the size of the bond issue for same to be placed on the November ballot. He woke refreshed at nine-thirty when she took his arm and whispered, "Wake up, Pat!" and walked her down Pine Avenue to the house.

"Elvira, I better—"

"Come in, Pat, I won't bite you."

She did not bite, but she did not let him go until three a.m. Punch wondered how long one man could sustain her; the thought was not forensic. He stopped at the café for a steak and three glasses of milk, fell into bed at four a.m., and did not wake until the town siren screeched the noon hour. Could he catch a train before Ossie came looking for him? He shaved, dressed, and was starting to pack when steps rang on the stairs and Ossie called:

"Wake up, Pat. You'll miss the parade!"

Number 37 made the Ophelia stop on the advertised, dropped Badger's boxcar in the hole, picked up, and steamed on. Badger led the chestnut to the ground, asked a yardman directions to the nearest livery barn, rode west on Railroad Street into a day of searching for a man who was probably two thousand miles away, lost forever, and the first thing he saw in the right front stall was a stocking-legged sorrel. It could not be! The barnman took the chestnut's rein.

"Overnight?"

"Yes—nice-looking sorrel there."

"He's for sale."

"Barn horse?"

"No, man rode him in last week."

"Where can I find him?"

"You passed it, the Rosebud, his name's Pat O'Doul."

Badger shouldered his bedroll and saddlebags, took the south side of Railroad Street, drew opposite the Rosebud Hotel as two men came outside and swung north around the corner; one was tall, broken-nosed, tin-eared! First the horse, now the rider? Mike had a phrase that fitted such luck: "Along toward morning the blind pig found an acorn." Badger crossed the street, entered the Rosebud Hotel, signed the register, asked the clerk if that wasn't Pat O'Doul who just left. The clerk nodded and gave him the key to Number 8, mentioned that O'Doul was in 6 but gone for the afternoon, the parade and contests. Badger grinned, went upstairs to 8, opened the door, placed his bedroll and saddlebags inside, closed the door, went up the hall and tried his skeleton key in 6. It worked easily, he closed the door behind him, saw the blanket roll on the bed, ready to pack and strap.

He searched the roll, bed, closet and dresser, looked
outside the window under the sill, behind the mirror,
found nothing, no money, no necklace. But Punch
would never leave cash in his room, and one of the
others must have the necklace. Badger locked the
door behind him, went to 8, washed face and hands,
changed shirts, and headed uptown. He came onto
the main street, Swiftwater, at the west end and
worked his way east through the crowd, saw Punch
and the other man, now joined by a woman, in front
of a drugstore on the south side. They must be local
people, their faces made them brother and sister, he
saw the woman's right hand lace into Punch's left; fast
worker, that Punch. No love-'em-and-leave-'em man;
he loved and killed. A boy hanging on the awning
irons let out a yell:

"Here they come!"

Badger heard the distant music, recognized the
opening bars of "Semper Fidelis." Dogs racing madly
in front, sunlight glinting on instruments and splendid
dress uniforms, the Ophelia silver cornet band led the
parade west on Swiftwater Street from the assembly
point in front of the Lutheran church. Behind the
band rode the grand marshal on a prancing Arabian,
followed by a magnificent red and gold pumper
pulled by four matched dapple grays, then two ladder
wagons, six hose carts, two more pumpers, another
band, pretty girls on floats, a drum and bugle corps,
GAR veterans, and the visiting volunteer fire de-
partments; a parade dear to small towns where everyone knew everyone else, even the dogs refrained
from fighting and the children clapped hands to the
beat and made faces at one another across the street.
All marched past Badger who watched Punch and
asked himself: when is the right time, where is the
right place, will he talk? And then, his uncle's voice:
kill them!

The crowd shifted, broke, moved north along the
avenues. Punch and his new-found friends rode the
human wave, Badger swam behind into the fair-

grounds grandstand, took a seat three rows above
them. On the bridge plank platform erected just
across the racetrack, the announcer tipped up a mon-
strous megaphone on a swivel post and welcomed
the crowd to the festivities. Badger watched foot
races, cart races, hose coupling races, ladder climbing,
demonstrations of rescue work, caring for injured,
treating burns; then the cover was removed from a
pit dug in the racetrack perpendicular to the grandstand, sixteen feet long, eight feet wide, four feet
deep, filled with a mud mixture that looked down-
right evil. The announcer introduced the eight finalists, the twenty-man teams dressed in old clothes and
caulked boots. The leadoff pair took positions facing
across the pit; a new two-inch manila rope was carefully stretched between them. The judge raised his
revolver, "Ready—Set—Bang!" and the tug of war
was on. People around Badger talked about the team
on the left, troopers from the regiment stationed at
Fort Robinson. The troopers won that opening match
in four minutes and three seconds; other pairs followed, tugged, won or took mud baths until, as an-
ticipated, the two favorites, Ophelia and troopers,
faced in the championship. The revolver barked,
the yellow rope twanged like a banjo string, at nine
minutes and twelve seconds the troopers used a cadence-count movement of give-yank-pull-snap to throw
the Ophelia anchorman momentarily off balance. Before he replanted his two hundred and eighty pounds,
he was flying through the air after his teammates,
and the troopers had finally won a war.

Badger followed the throng from the fairgrounds
along the street to the east side of town where the
standpipe towered on four steel legs, overshadowing
the baseball park on the south and the high school on
the north. The avenue in front of school, standpipe,
and ball park was blocked off, restraining ropes were
erected around the dampened arena; the crowd
rolled down both sides and crowded against the ropes,
eager for the day's feature, an event as savage and

dangerous as a bullfight, as intimate as two gladiators on the sand. The weapons were in place: from two freshly painted hydrants at the ends, two new white hoses ran across the earth to two brass nozzles tilted muzzles-up on wood blocks, on the baselines one hundred and fifty feet apart. In the center, seventy-five feet from each nozzle, was a small, cone-shaped pedestal. No bull, no spears, daggers, swords, nets, tridents, capes, suits of light, horns, pics, or sticks; but those nozzles manned by experts and charged with full water pressure, could defeat gladiator, bullfighter, and bull, at the same time, in close battle. The experts were firemen, specifically one nozzleman and one back man, two teams of two men, soon to engage in a water fight. No one had to warn the crowd to stay behind the restraining ropes; water pressure was so strong that, should a nozzle break loose, it was clearly understood that anyone accidentally injured or killed had to take care of his/her own doctor or undertaker bills.

The nozzleman faced forward, protected by the back man who faced him. The back man was always big; if agile too, he became a force to reckon with. The nozzleman directed movement orally, with head jerks, and movement of the nozzle. They wore firefighting clothes, helmets, and hip boots. They started on the baselines. Procedure might vary from one town to another, but the general outline of the water fight was the same. A field judge stationed on the standpipe-pumper side walked to the center and placed the ball—usually rubber-coated leather similar to a medicine ball, thirty-six inches in diameter—on the cone-shaped pedestal. He returned to his post; on the opposite side, atop the plank tower, stood referee and timer. A water fight lasted five minutes; during the opening two minutes pressure was maintained at one-half, increased to two-thirds for the third and fourth minutes, and opened to full pressure for the final minute. Firemen could not take the physical buffeting of more than one fight a day, so eliminations were held in the various towns over a period of two or three months, to determine the two finalists.

This was the idealistic picture of a water fight; the human equations were as many and varied as there were clever, devious, scheming firemen whose one aim in life on that one afternoon was washing the enemy down the gutter. When the gun sounded, the hydrants opened, and both teams advanced on the ball, it was not unusual for both streams of water to strike the ball simultaneously. When this occurred, the ball rose a few inches and hung, dancing, spangled in water, the opening movement of a ballet, then flew wherever dominant force decreed. Whoever drove the ball across the other team's baseline won the fight.

Six steps behind Punch on the east side of the street, Badger learned from the excited talk that the O'Neal Shamrocks had been undefeated, undisputed champions of the sandhill country for five years. Their nozzleman was a redheaded Irishman, his back man was a huge, agile, black-haired Irishman, their cheering section was a solid block on the west side of the street, making more noise than the tower of Babel on a windy day. Despite the Shamrocks' unquestioned ability, the O'Neal rooters had screamed foul all summer, swearing that the new Ophelia nozzleman was not a legal resident. The Ophelia Fire Department went into district court and proved that he had moved to Ophelia the previous autumn. No matter O'Neal presented proof that he had been the finest nozzleman on the Omaha Fire Department, he stated under oath that he had a good job, liked the sandhill climate, intended to stay in Ophelia. He was standing now on his baseline, with his back man, facing the O'Neal Shamrocks, watching the field judge place the ball on the pedestal and return to the east sideline. On the tower, the referee mouthed his megaphone.

"Standpipe full?"

"All full!"

"Start the pumper!"

The big red and gold pumper added its powerful thrust to the water pressure surging through the main to the hydrants.

"Ophelia, are you ready?"

"Ready!"

"O'Neal, are you ready?"

"Ready!"

The referee raised his revolver, the timer placed a big thumb on the gnarled crown of his Horse Timer watch. Badger reached his decision based on circumstance, time and opportunity. He went forward as the referee began his count

"One!"

and spoke to Punch's right ear: "Killing her next, Punch?"

"Two!"

and backed away as Punch stiffened, but did not turn.

"Bang!"

Punch jumped an inch, the woman on his left felt his tenseness through their clasped hands. The hydrant wrenches spun, water rushed through the opened valves into the hoses, crowd roar drowned all lesser sounds. Badger watched Punch, would he break? Where would he go if he did break? Would he tell where the others were, who they were? The fight was on, brutal and vicious, the Irish had met their match in strength, guile and deceit, yet held their own. The Ophelia nozzleman was of English descent; could the Irish do other? The woman looked up and spoke urgently to Punch, but he could not hear her, stood rigidly in place, watching the fight. Two minutes, three, the four-minute mark approached. Ophelia was forced back within thirty feet of its baseline, the visiting Irish on the west sideline were bellowing for another Clontarf, whatever that was, the field judge caught the timer's wave and gave the signal for full pressure. Something had to break. Badger willed the man in front of him: you, do some-

thing, don't stand there like a post! The ball was
rolling, skipping, the Irish were groaning, the Shamrocks retreated, braced, stood before their baseline.
The ball hung between streams, dancing, trembling,
as Badger moved forward and spoke in Punch's ear:

"Where did Snapper go, Punch? Tell me, it'll go
easier on you!"

The ball was spinning in spray, sunlight flashing
in prismatic colors. Punch spun, threw the woman
against her brother, for a lonely moment Punch and
Badger were the only humans on the wet street.
Punch saw Badger, eyes and skin, knew who Badger
was, not his name, but who he was. Recognition and
fear were in the china-blue eyes, the broken nose
that twitched as Punch backed off. The woman cried,
"Pat!" Punch bumped into others, whirled, ducked
under the restraining rope, ran with hell on his heels
across the street through the final seconds of the
water fight. His instinct was working, he was going
to make it! The Irish nozzleman caught a heel, lost
his balance for one precious moment, involuntarily
pushed the rear of his nozzle down, the muzzle rose,
the stream of water overshot the ball, gave the
Ophelia nozzleman the chance he had patiently
awaited. He shifted his full-bore blast from ball to
men, hammered under the tilted Irish stream, knocked
the back man head-under-heels, the somersaulting
body took the nozzleman along, their nozzle flew into
the air, became a striking snake, brass head and
white hose body whipping wildly. Punch was two
steps from breaking through the danger zone when
the loose nozzle lashed out, struck the ball, drove it
squarely into Punch's face like a gigantic boxing glove
delivering the knockout of all time; in the same
breath, as the revolver shot ended the fight and the
hydrant men frantically closed the valves, the Ophelia
nozzleman drove the ball across the O'Neal baseline.
Ophelia was the new champion of the sandhills, and
a visiting stranger lay in the street.

Badger had a feeling; it ran through him so strongly

that he did not wait. He slipped through the crowd to the next street south, ran west, turned south again to Railroad, reached the livery barn gasping for breath. Uncle Bad Knees was saying, "Maybe you should try overalls!" and Badger read the card hung on the office door: "Rear doors open, gone to water fight." Badger trotted back to the Rosebud Hotel, found a similar card on the desk, took the stairs three at a jump, opened his door, scooped up his bedroll and saddlebags, went down on the run, dropped his key on the register, and kept running west on Railroad around the livery barn to the back fence. He climbed over, ran through the open doorway, saddled the chestnut, tied on his gear, and led him into the corral behind the barn. He heard the front doors squeal open, the barnmen were back from the fight, voices hoarse with excitement.

"My god, he was dead before he hit the ground!"

"Hey, you see that series score?"

"Who cares—neck broken, think of that!"

"Well, I care. Overall pitched one helluva game."

"Wonder where he was from?"

"The Cubs sure showed the Tigers."

Badger opened the back gate and mounted.

"I heard the marshal tell his boys to get down here and guard his room."

"Why, you s'pose?"

"Oh, they always do that in accidental death—"

Badger rode in a wide circle around Ophelia to the east, came back onto the road, let the chestnut set the pace. Punch was dead. Uncle Bad Knees kept floating in and out of mind's-eye, face dark with disapproval. His nephew had found Punch, frightened him—great god, had he frightened him!—now Punch was dead and where were the other three?

5

Badger stopped at a farm on the Keya Paha near Wewala Crossing and had a mess of roasted potatoes and tender young rabbit with an armless man and his one-legged wife. He told Badger that he had been a night watchman in a whiskey warehouse in Moline, Illinois, a sustentative job in spring, summer and fall, but pure arctic misery in winter. He had an eight-gauge punt gun mounted on an iron hitching post in front of his barrel chair facing the only entrance; his big toes hooked into two oversized butt rings controlled aim and movement while he fired by pulling the trigger cords with his teeth. He had never been able to keep his toes from freezing.

Badger said, "How did you lose your arms?"

The armless man and his first wife ran trotters on the Three-I circuit and won their fair share of purses, but one afternoon in Decatur, three lengths in front of the field, his sulky fell apart. He lit face down in the middle of the track and, before he could curl, three sets of wheels ran over his outstretched arms.

"Then you took the night watchman's job?"

"No. Sold the trotters, bought a string of pacers."

And invented a trick seat that enabled him to keep his boots firmly in the irons while grasping the reins in his teeth. He was doing nicely until his wife met a fully armed man who persuaded her to sell the pacers and run off. That shook the armless man's faith in

gaited stock. He was grumping around his cousin's
house in Port Byron, the steamboat pilot's town above
Moline, when he met his second wife, who had lost
her left leg during a lively youth. She was calling on a
man with whom she was enamored when his wife
came home unexpectedly; she jumped out the bedroom window, forgot it was on the second story,
and broke her right leg on the cellar door. Kindly
passersby carried her to the nearest sawbones, who
set her leg, but his bottle slipped while he worked
and he cut her left leg; only a scratch but his instruments were filthy, sepsis set in, and by the time she
got to a clean, sober physician, her left leg had to
be cut off. She retired to her sister's farm outside Port
Byron and waited patiently while her right leg
knitted, her left stump healed, and her sister's husband carved a wooden leg. She met the armless man
over the apple-bobbing tub at the Woodman of the
World Halloween party, and it did appear they
were fated to entwine what they still possessed and
present a whole front to the world. They were doing
well, he as night watchman, she learning to walk, but
he could not solve the frostbite problem, his teeth
started giving him trouble, so they came west and
loved the farm except for one fault.

"What's that?"

"I can't stop talking the ears off my visitors."

Badger looked at them and doffed his hat. They
were brave, foolhardy people and he wished for a
dozen friends like them.

"Regret anything?"

"Not me, but she wants something."

His wife spoke for the first time: "I'd dearly love a
separator."

"How many cows are you milking?"

"Four."

"What do you do now?"

"Set and skim."

Badger said, "Hang onto those cows," and rode for
Eddie Malone's farm south of Gregory, found Eddie

waiting on Ponca Creek with hot food in a burlap-covered dishpan and news from Otto Ott. Otto and Louie Allard had cold-nosed Snapper's trail west of Turtle Butte on a course for Bull Creek that swung abruptly through the Bijou Hills toward the Missouri. Did that give him any ideas?

Badger had racked his brains on the long ride, trying to guess where Snapper was headed; now he told Eddie it appeared likely that Snapper and the people in the wagon might be closing on a rendezvous. Did that make sense?

"Sure, but where?"

"Want to think some more on it."

"Dream on it, rest this horse."

Badger crawled into Eddie's wagon and slept six hours in warm blankets on sweet straw. Eddie woke him at ten, hung the lantern on a box cleat, and brought the chestnut in from grass. Badger drank coffee, ate sandwiches, hoisted himself into the saddle.

"Eddie, I'm going to Fairview, head for the river, try to pick up that wagon track."

"One ought to lead to the other."

"Will you wire Mike, have my team and wagon ready?"

Badger rode due east, came over the ridge and down the big draw past the stockyards into Fairview at nine o'clock the next morning. He found Andaman Littlefield in Mike's swivel chair with her nose in a book. She had discarded her ragged kersey cap and sheepherder's outfit for a pair of old Levi's, moccasins, pullover sweater and blue shirt, collar hidden under a flood of yellow hair.

"What you reading?"

"Bowditch—you're late."

"Late?"

"Mike expected you at sunup."

Badger began laughing. Ride a brave horse more than one hundred miles, meet armless, one-legged, and other interesting people, the one before him named for a bunch of islands in the Bay of Bengal, and find Bowditch, the seaman's bible, in the middle of the continent. Captain Horatio Perriwinkle had once spent an entire evening telling Badger what Bowditch meant to deep-sea sailors, but to Missouri River steamboat captains and pilots, on the lookout for deadheads, sandbars, and mean Indians, Bowditch was an unshot sextant. That did not mean he was dry reading; to the contrary, he gave landlubbers insane dreams about salt water and the Spanish Main. Andaman Littlefield would probably volunteer to find the lost wagon with her compass and a hairpin. Badger suddenly realized she was watching him under lashes so long they looked as if she'd snipped them off a raccoon. Yellow hair, black lashes, dark brown Portugee eyes. She closed the book with a bang.

"Mike's waiting."

And followed him out to the chestnut, made another of her cow-jumped-over-the-moon leaps behind him, kept her mouth shut during the brief ride up the alley into the yard where Mike was hitching the paints to the shining clean wagon. She slid off and ran into the house while Badger dismounted stiffly and gave Mike a hand; snapping traces, he told Mike what had happened in Ophelia, not sparing himself, admitting he had guessed wrong.

"Why?"

"Punch broke and ran."

"That's what you wanted."

"Before he told me anything!"

"Was he the right man?"

"Yes."

"Then you guessed right. He's dead. You're on the track. Find that wagon, it'll lead you to Snapper."

"Will you tell Uncle?"

"Already sent word—" they watched Andaman come from the house with a bulging sack "—her father's in town today and tomorrow, pulling teeth. Will you drop her off at their place?"

"How much did you tell her?"

"Just enough—" she clambered over the front wheel onto the seat, stowed the sack between her legs, and grabbed the reins "—mind what I told you, Andy."

"Yes, Mike."

"Henry, let her drive. You need sleep and she needs the practice."

Badger crawled painfully under the tarp onto the blankets spread over the hay. She said, "Rhumatiz? Giddap!" and the paints were so surprised at her contralto they stepped out like a pair of fire horses. Badger closed his eyes and slept the entire jolting, twisting ride until the tailgate opened, hands helped him down, led him inside somewhere and pushed him down on a cot. She went back outside and spoke to the paints, her voice fading as she led them off into silence. Badger slept, smelled coffee, cracked one eye, saw yellow lamplight pooled on a round oak table.

"Where—what time?"

"Our place, ten o'clock."

Badger sat up, pawed the floor with his socks. Where were his boots? She pointed a fork.

"I took 'em off—hungry?"

"Behind time."

"You can't find wagon tracks in the dark."

"I can get to where I can find them in the light."

He pulled on his boots, stuck the laces under the tongues, went outside, felt the cold wind and smelled the night, came back squinting against the lamplight, followed the sweep of her arm to the washstand, soaped and rinsed, washed sleep from his eyes.

"Mike says you know the river better'n anybody."

"Maybe."

He dried, buttoned his shirt, took the chair offered. She served eggs, ham, late Hubbard squash, and rhubarb pie with a sweet-sour taste his uncle would love. My god! He was starting to think the way she talked, as if everything was possible. His uncle and this girl?

"Another piece?"

"Thanks."

"Still want to start tonight?"

"Don't want to, got to."

She brought the sack to the table and shook out his freshly washed clothes. "Listen, you want me to—" she saw his face and raised both arms "—don't say it! I've got no business traipsing off with you, and my mother only dead these twelve years, excuse me, I didn't mean that the way it sounded."

"The hell you never."

"Well, all right, I did."

"Sure you did, I say things like that, and I mean every damn word. I'd like to have you along, I think you could help, but not on this stretch. Looking for sign is a one-man job. Besides, you've got sheep to watch."

"Yes, damn it! Why do people have to work?"

"Tell me when you find out. Where can I change clothes?"

"Come out when you're ready."

She lit a barn lantern and left the house. He heard her dog for the first time that night, giving her a soft whuff of assurance. Badger took off his fancy-dan outfit and stuffed it into the sack, put on his clean-smelling old clothes, laced up his boots, and followed her outside. She came from the barn leading the paints, already hitched up and pulling the wagon, and held them while he climbed onto the seat. She wiggled her lantern at the wagon box.

"You've got everything in there but a mermaid. I know most of it, but the label's smeared on one bottle. I think it says pearls, but I never saw a blue pearl."

"The label reads p - e - r - l - e, forty to a bottle, methylene blue compound."

"Oh, them! My father says they ain't worth a hoot."

"They're none of your business."

"Why not? My father says that any man who starts celebrating in a strange bedroom with a p - e - r - l - e, usually ends up with a c - l - a - p. You think I want any truck with a man who uses those things? I know

you don't. Mike told me you carry that medicine box
in case somebody needs help."

She was a year younger than Amelie, she knew too
much, or was it too little, she didn't care about his
mixed blood, acted as if she'd forgotten he told her
the day they met. That could be the Portugee in her.
Her father must be a rare type to let his seventeen-
year-old daughter go cavorting off in the night with a
mixed-blood, no matter Mike's glowing testimonials.
Badger wanted to meet Littlefield, the man who read
books while his cattle ran away, weaned his daughter
on methylene blue, and pulled teeth so he could
bother his patients with homesick stories about Cape
Porpus, Maine.

"Thanks, Andy."

"You're welcome, Henry. Good luck."

Long after her lantern faded under the earth's
curve, Badger remembered her face; then night en-
gulfed him as the paints walked the road until he
sensed the time to swing toward the river. Dawn
found him on the South Scalp Creek trail, bumping
through the river bluffs; at midday he turned north on
the river road of the Brulé war parties. Flinty pony
hoofs no longer pulverized the grass, in a few years
the present would cover yesterday and future eyes
would never know that warriors rode here. Badger
had to ax his way through the worst undergrowth,
shovel the steepest landslides, push cutbanks into
the washouts. No horse or wagon track was fresher
than last year's dust; could the wagon driver have
laid far out to the west and gone north on a parallel
course? If so, it had to be someone who knew the
river country as intimately as he did.

Badger camped on North Scalp Creek, shook frost
from the tarp, poured kerosene to start his breakfast
fire. Late that day he reached Whetstone Creek
where the river bluffs lay a mile back from the channel; at the mouth of Whetstone Creek below the is-
land the flood plain was a quarter-mile wide, densely
overgrown with willows and vines, but the second

terrace was good land if worked up. In '68 the Indian Department had laid out the first Brulé Agency on that second terrace land north of the creek and prepared two thousand acres for the farm machinery shipped upriver at great expense. Nothing remained but rotted walls and one mixed-blood family living in the only decent house; looking down the widening creek toward the river, Badger asked himself how he could conceal signs of crossing if he came from the south. There was only one way.

He drove downstream to the shallows, took off his boots and socks, rolled up his overalls and underwear, led the paints off the low bank into the water, circled the quicksand bar, dodged the soft spots, walked up the north bank under the trees. Dressing, he drove upstream until he saw where the bank had been broken down by a team pulling a big wagon from the creek. He followed faint wheel tracks toward the bluffs until more horses joined, walked down that backtrail to the creek where the horses had climbed from the water and angled across the second terrace to join the wagon. To verify the beginning, all he need do was follow the south bank upstream until he found where they tied float logs to the wagon, drove it and the string of horses into the center of Whetstone Creek, and came downstream into shallow water before leaving by the north bank. Somebody did know the country as intimately as Uncle Bad Knees and his nephew. If the nephew had been a week later with October racing into the moon of the hairless calves, all signs would have been obliterated.

Badger made camp under the bluffs and followed the trail next morning, north toward Dry Creek and the Bijou Hills, inspecting ridgelines and hilltops for tracks left by anyone scouting campsites and keeping an eye on the backtrail. He found their first campsite, made his own nearby, found manure where the six horses had been picketed on the grass, four on long lines, two on short; the team was on long neck lines behind the wagon, hair tufts on the brush were bay, the wagon tracks fitted Uncle Bad Knees' width. Badger could not measure the exact tire width; weather had crumbled the edges. He found footprints where they walked toes down, weight on heels, two and three slow steps, then stopped and listened like hunters. One was a big, heavyset man, the smaller prints almost like a boy's; both gave him the odd feeling they were Sioux, made him remember the old Sioux legend and half-expect to find a badger along their trail. The Sioux respected the badger deeply. Strong and quick, the badger could bite deeply. The old legend said if a warrior killed a badger, turned it on its back, cut it open at the chest and removed the insides without losing the blood, then looked into the blood as it thickened, and saw his own image as he was then, he would die young. But if he saw an old man with white hair, he would have long life, could take risks, count coups, and die with a cane in his hand.

Three days later he was in the Bijou Hills, coming down Bull Creek toward White River, following a fading trail rapidly losing identity under wind, rain and spent time. He located the campsite on the east bank, five miles from the creek mouth; in a cold fall rain he slipped and slid through the mud, waded the creek, found a set of hoofprints coming from the west into the water. He counted seven horses picketed on the grass behind the cottonwoods; the campsite gave up tea leaves, coffee grounds, eggshells, ax marks where wood was chopped, two cigar butts, potato peels, three peach cans, and an empty whiskey bottle. Finally, between firebed and wagon, a third set of footprints, sized between the other two. Was the newcomer named Snapper, was the horse a black?

The trail crossed Bull Creek and went downstream to the mouth where White River ran between steep bluffs toward the Missouri; turned west, vanished, reappeared here and there, a yard of wagon track, a footprint, six horses crossing a low, damp spot under trees. Where was the seventh horse? Further upstream he identified the bay team, wagon, and original occupants; came to the gooseneck bend, drove the paints down the approach on the run, splashed across the reef rock, stopped on the north bank to find the trail. Hopeless! Blotted out by many teams and wagons headed in all directions: northeast toward Chamberlin, north and northwest to any of half a dozen stops on the Milwaukee Railroad which crossed the Missouri at Chamberlin and followed Medicine Creek west along the general gradient of the old Chamberlin–Black Hills wagon road. Badger took the road north to a whistle stop where nobody remembered a horse and wagon outfit; put paints and wagon in the livery barn, caught the next eastbound train to Chamberlin, and satisfied himself that Snapper had not been in town. He returned to the whistle stop, drove west to the next town, where the depot agent remembered the whole shebang: wagon with a white duck top, big bay team, six horses on lead, rolled up from the south just after supper.

"How many people?"

"Three."

"Get a good look at them?"

"Too dark, just the one bought the stockcar space to Vivian."

"What was he like?"

"Roundish sort of feller, not so tall as he was wide."

"See a black horse in the string?"

"No black horse."

Badger loaded the paints and wagon into a stockcar, rode west to Vivian, pulled off the dock and tied up behind the depot. The agent had been home when the early freight spotted the stockcar in question; nobody uptown remembered Snapper, but the clerk in the general store had just opened up and swept out when a heavyset man bought two sackfuls of groceries. Badger returned to the depot. The agent had not sold stockcar space or passenger tickets to anyone answering those general descriptions. Pierre lay due north. The agent saw him off.

"Some election, huh?"

"Who won?"

"Man, where you been? Taft won!"

"Bully for him."

Badger drove north, looked for sign, but time and the weather had washed out all tracks. Still, he knew where that seventh horse was: back where Bull Creek entered White River, somebody had led the black horse downstream, fired a shot, and watched it tumble into the current. The wagon outfit and three people were somewhere near Pierre, getting ready to— what were they doing, what would they try next?

Brown's final warning was get ready to feel small, no jokes intended, because that was how the Sioux described the grassland west of the Missouri. A man could ride all day and nothing seemed to move; not the man, not his horse, not time itself. Or so it felt, once Snapper left Gregory behind and moved into the grass under the cold October sun with the wind on his face. A man could ride his life away along the streams toward distant buttes, past waterholes over ridges into wide valleys that led loping coyotes and lobo wolves through lost horizons. Cattle, horses, animals; wind, sun, stars; cold food, no fires, until Snapper saw Turtle Butte on his left front and felt like Columbus discovering America.

He circled Turtle Butte into the Bijou Hills and rode east until he saw twin buttes spiral upward on his right hand; turned ninety degrees north and rode half a day, turned forty-five degrees west and rode out the balance of that day, the night, and the following morning. At sunrise he turned hard east, watched for a horseshoe-shaped ridge, open toes facing him, rode between them over the heel into the creek valley, saw smoke rising from the cottonwoods. He splashed across the creek and found them waiting; the girl took his reins, slipped the cinches, dumped saddle and roll, led the black horse away. Brown helped lug the gear to the fire, poured coffee that

burned Snapper's tongue while his teeth chattered
Dixie on the tin rim. He swore softly and grinned at
Brown.

"Save you the asking—no trouble."

Brown poked the fire; sparks flew, frizzled the hair
on the back of his right hand. Brown had changed
from the summer roly-poly to a harder, wider-looking
man, teeth whiter against growing beard and darken-
ing skin. He wore a fur cap, scarf and an elkskin shirt
under a pair of tick-striped overalls, legs wrapped in
leggings that stretched from moccasins to well above
his knees.

"Who saw you, Snapper?"

"Rubes."

"How do you feel?"

"Cold, hungry."

"We can warm you, feed you, but you got to say
when you're ready to ride."

"Say when, Trader."

"I will. First, we got to shed that black horse."

Snapper spread his bedroll on the tarp beside the
wagon, slept while the girl cooked supper, woke at
Brown's call and ate wolfishly; slept again until he
woke on a morning so cold he heard the girl crack ice
to draw water. He rode on the wagon with Brown,
across the creek and downstream to the mouth at
White River, held the reins while Brown cut the
black horse from the string and led it along the bluffs,
slipped the halter and shot in one motion; the black
tumbled down the bluff face into the water, rolled
over twice, and disappeared. Brown came back to the
wagon, drove upstream along White River, crossed
on a reef rock ford that slabbed beneath the current,
the girl leading the string, following the wagon up the
bank in the neck of the bend, on north across the
grass to a whistle stop on the Milwaukee Railroad,
where Brown bought space west to Vivian. When
the next freight train stopped, they loaded into a
stockcar, rode sixty-odd miles to Vivian, unloaded
across the implement dock and tied up behind the

depot while Brown walked uptown to buy groceries.
Snapper stayed on the wagon seat, the girl crouched
on the buckskin, two shapeless lumps in cold, gray
dawn.

"You cold, kid?"

"What you think?"

"I'm cold, but I ain't as young and healthy as you."

"I ain't so young."

"That's not my drift, kid. I mean you can go all
day and night, bat your eyes, and go some more. Me?
I'd be with you till we batted eyes, then I'd be flat
on my back from the exercise."

She laughed, a funny shrilling sound that welled
up in her throat and ended in a grunt as she yanked
the sheepskin closer around her neck. Brown came
treading through the watery dawn mist with two big
sacks of groceries, they drove north for an hour before halting to feed the horses and boil coffee. The girl
went for water while Brown spread his map and
showed Snapper why they had taken the freight
train west: the river from Pierre to Chamberlin flowed
mostly eastward, they were now due south of the capital. The short train ride had saved many hard-driv-
ing miles. Brown folded the map, lit a cigar, and
grinned at Snapper.

"Rose likes you."

"I tickle her funny bone."

"You made her laugh, Snapper."

"That it, that tongue-twister?"

"She heard me coming, let me know it was all
right."

"Well goddamn—!"

"Oh hell, not you, Snapper. Just habit with us. Part
of her won't never be civilized enough to tie on an
apron. That was a Sioux laugh you heard. The day
she giggles like some silly bitch in the Pierre parlor,
that's the day I'll know she's finally threw her sticks."

"Sticks?"

"Sticks, stones, bones, beads, whatever her omens
are. She don't count on prayer books and crosses.

She's cut up the middle and quartered to boot. That don't make for easy living."

"What bloods, Trader?"

"Me, I'm French, Cree, Sans Arc. Rose's mother was French and Two Kettle Sioux."

"How old is she?"

"Just past eighteen."

"That's young."

"Out here, with no man, that's old as the hills."

"How come, Trader?"

"Snapper, I don't force her. Never! She wants to go, I say go. She wants to do, I say do. She went to mission school awhile, they said be this, do that, wear this, forget that. You don't win no races riding side-saddle. She went home to her grandfather, when she got older she started coming with me."

"Easy to see one reason why. She's got good hands."

"Wish you could see inside her, tell her the right way."

"She looks all right to me, Trader."

"Only one sure end."

"Christ, you're bad as Punch! Always looking on the dark side."

"Punch was nobody's fool, Snapper."

"Yes, his own, and how come you say *was?*"

"Got a feeling."

"Scratch it, Trader. He'll be waiting for me in Seattle."

They drove from one creek valley to another, followed low ridges, came down along Bad River to Fort Pierre on the last day of October, went into camp in the cottonwoods that lined the bottoms on the west side of the Missouri. Election was Tuesday, November 3rd, so it was a waste of time to transact business until the votes were cast. Brown opened a big deer-skin clothes case and tossed out an elkskin shirt with ratty, gnawed fringes and a high-crowned, sweat-blotched old Stetson. He made Snapper dress for size; the hat was fine, the shirt loose, with the long shirt and high crown Snapper looked half a foot tall-

er. His lined, seamed face was so weathered that his
skin matched most breeds, but Rose mixed up a dye
and rubbed it into his forehead and neck for more
effect. Brown tied a deep purple kerchief around his
neck and gave him a pair of leather gauntlets.

"What you think now, Rose?"

"If he don't talk loud."

They went into Fort Pierre on Monday, bought
groceries and whiskey, stood listening to the gossip
while Rose looked at the goods in the showcase. Her
face had that flat, sliding look Snapper had noticed
when he rejoined them on Bull Creek; a slick, smooth
surface that caught nothing and gave off nothing, the
features losing compliance in the blankness of the
look itself. Rose had her thoughts locked in a doorless
vault stronger than any safe. Snapper walked over
and stood beside her, stared through the finger-
smudged plate glass at the worthless doodads.

"Anything look good, kid?"

"No."

"Let's buy some lemon drops."

"Let's go home."

They returned to camp and stayed put until Wednesday morning, sleeping and eating, doing the
chores, having a few drinks, never getting drunk,
never trying to walk the chalk line. Rose cooked,
tended the horses, slipped away between meals and
went up in smoke. Snapper wondered what she
did and Brown said she always walked beside rivers,
he had no idea why, whatever it was made her feel
better. On Wednesday morning Brown said, "Keep an
eye on things, Rose," and took Snapper into Fort
Pierre where they heard that Taft had licked Bryan.
"All right," Brown said. "Let's go look at a horse."

He took Snapper across the river and gave what
he called a booster's oration on the beauties and
blessings of Pierre, the magnet for all the trash west
of Chicago and north of Kansas City. Why, only a
few short years ago, most of the steady population
did nothing but drink, gamble and loaf. When the

legislature was in session, the politicians and lobbyists swarmed into town, roosted in the two-dollar-a-day hotels, ate big meals, drank barrels of whiskey and made endless speeches, but never seemed to pass any laws but those naming the state flower, putting a bounty on wolves, and declaring another holiday so they could use their year-round passes from the North Western and Milwaukee Railroads. Brown said, "They never stop jawing," and turned Snapper down Missouri Avenue where forgotten hosts of fallen angels, working in Jud's, Hallie's, Maud's, and Molly's entertained the lonely bachelors during long winter months and, like all valuable livestock, were inspected regularly by their own doctor, a woman who took care of them exclusively. There were only two kinds of women in the capital city; wives and sporting ladies. Wives didn't go out much at night, but if they did, they carried long hatpins and .22 revolvers for protection against the drunks. Brown shrugged expressively.

"But all that was long ago!"

"Oh sure, Trader!"

They left Missouri Avenue, took a footpath around the hill shoulder, approached a farm set in the deep shadow of trees facing the river. Brown said, "Wait here," and crossed from the barn to the back porch, knocked on the kitchen door. The door opened an inch, he spoke to someone inside and returned to the barn.

"Your friend bashful or ugly, Trader?"

"He's one of them albinos, can't stand light, but sure can smell a score from hell to breakfast."

"Anybody can smell, Trader. How does he score?"

"See for yourself."

A tall, white-haired man in a black suit came from the house and crossed the farmyard, legs moving elastically, black-gloved hands manipulating a malacca cane and holding a dark gray, wide-brimmed felt hat between eyes and sun. He wore black congress gaiters, black string tie on a blue shirt, and a gold-linked watch chain across the soft blue waistcoat showing its white piping inside his coat. When he stopped before them, Snapper saw the riding bow spectacles tight on his long, knife-blade nose, looked through the smoked coquille lenses and recognized the pink, colorless eyes of the pure albino.

"Snapper, this is Whitey Crosier."

Whitey's gloved hand was firm, his voice strong. "Please to meet you at last, Snapper. I saw you ride."

"Where?"

"Last time in New Orleans, a red mare in a filly race. As I recollect, you won by seven going away."

"Nine. She was a good mare."

"Then you'll be happy to meet another."

Whitey Crosier opened the padlock on the side door hasp, led them between the grain and tack rooms across the center alley to the center box stall. The barn windows were shaded with tinted cheese-cloth that diluted the outer light and painted a soft aura over the horse in the stall. Whitey Crosier extended his left hand, the mare took the sugar and blew her thanks. Whitey said, "Say hello to Snapper, Flop Ears."

Brown came from the tack room with his arms full of gear. Whitey opened the stall and led the mare into the alley, rubbed her neck while Snapper moved around her, sizing her conformation. Whitey seemed to read his mind:

"Going six, no faults, runs best at a little over eight hundred—"

"She goes eight?"

"Fooled you, eh?"

"Chest and barrel."

"Very solid, this little lady."

"How much work she had?"

"Not enough, Snapper. Please, saddle her, get her feel."

Brown said, "Your choice, Snapper," and extended two saddles, a plain English and a strong, lightweight park with a cloth-quilted serge pad, iron stirrups, and double girths.

"She used to both, Whitey?"

"Yes."

"Weights?"

"English runs six, park about nine."

"Let's try the park."

Brown handed Snapper a fine Navajo blanket. Snapper brushed the mare's back smooth, laid the blanket over, eased the park saddle on and let the girths dangle. He climbed the stall boards and stepped out on her like gossamer, instinctively lifting his knees to suit his toes to her, closed his teeth on an imaginary whip, bent forward and squinted between her flop ears, felt her gather under him. A perfect lady, fragile to the ignorant eye as a soda cracker, all steel and muscle to the knowing lover. A mouse-colored mare with flop ears, a thoroughbred runner with Arabian points and Morgan bottom, and something—a wisp from yesterday—that made Snapper think of Mexico.

"How long we got, Whitey?"

"Thanksgiving Day."

"What's the competition?"

"Blaze-faced sorrel racer."

"Owner?"

"Man named Pass Johnson."

Snapper scissored one leg and slid to the ground so smoothly the mare did not move.

"Gents, I bid you goodby."

Whitey Crosier unhooked his spectacles and wiped his red-rimmed eyes with a white kerchief.

"Why?"

"I rode in Texas, New Mexico, Arizona. Saw that man two, three times. Rancher, ain't he, PJ brand?"

"That's him."

"What's he doing up here?"

"Big reservation lease north of the Cheyenne."

"Look for me south of the Platte. That man don't

ever forget a skin deal, he gets even when he catches up, and he always catches up."

"Snapper, this is no skin deal."

"Whitey, how good is his horse?"

"Very good."

"But this mare can beat him?"

"With you up."

"Rider makes some difference. Not that much."

"Snapper, if we show you how, prove you're in no danger, will you stay?"

"When do I peek?"

"Day after tomorrow, Snapper. You'll get your first look at the way this race will be run."

6

Badger pulled into Flapjack Nellie's road ranch late that night and splashed through the icy drizzle to the house with Lester, the stable boy, plucking nervously at his coat and reminding him how mad Nellie got if anybody bothered her after the kitchen was closed. Badger crossed the back porch into the kitchen and stood dripping dirty water on the linoleum until Nellie came bullroaring from the parlor, saw him, and spent two minutes saying how blankety-blank glad she was to see him but where the hell had he been keeping himself the past year.

"Year and three months, Nellie. Lester didn't know me."

"Christ! wet as a drowned rat, I barely did. Get them clothes off."

"Nellie, you're prettier than ever."

"You lying bastard!"

"And I hope you found a new man."

"Henry, I swore off men."

"For keeps?"

"Until I get the urge. You want a bath first, or something to eat?"

"Bath."

"How'd you come?"

"Wagon."

Nellie shouted, "Lester, where are—oh, now listen,

take good care of Henry's team, Henry, you want
anything from your wagon?"

"Bedroll and a blue clothes bag."

"Hear that, Lester? Scoot!" Nellie closed the porch
door and went around the table to the hall. "The
cash customers are using the bathroom, Henry. Can
you make do here?"

"Sure, Nellie."

"You know where everything is, help yourself."

Nellie strode up the hallway toward the rackety din
of compatibility, a stocky little woman in a starched
daisy pattern housedress, green apron, black felt
boots, blue-visored cardsharp's cap yanked over her
red hair, burnt ends poking every which way, defy-
ing the curling irons that caused the original damage
and the hands that tried to rectify, callused hands
scarred from years of hot stove lids, popping grease,
and razor-sharp knives. She was scrupulously clean
in body, clothes, and kitchen, and a lifetime of hard
usage kept her vocal cords as rough as burlap sack-
ing. Nellie looked as mean as chastity locked in a
harem, gave and begged no quarter, preferred to de-
fend home and honor with a solid maple rolling pin.
She had cooked many years in Black Hills mining
and lumber camps before moving to Milo Smith's road
ranch twelve miles west of Fort Pierre; that was
ten years ago. Badger met her three months after
she arrived when he knocked on the kitchen door and
asked if he could buy a meal. Hat politely in hand,
head up, eyes meeting hers squarely; she understood
his youth, his blood, and no sign of apology for same
as he added bluntly:

"I'm part Indian."

"I'm part human," Nellie replied, "but I don't brag
about it. Come in."

"Smith don't—"

"Smith don't run my kitchen."

"Thank you."

"Glad for the company."

"Me too."

A lasting friendship began that day. Badger had never known a woman who spoke such plain language laced with so many old-fashioned cusswords, but he never once felt that Nellie talked dirty. Everything she did was natural, she had never entertained a dirty thought in her life. She had lived with many men, married one, and sure enough, she told Badger, "The sonofabitch wouldn't work a lick, just set around the kitchen eating, finally ran off with a bowlegged whore."

Nellie had a gleeful sense of humor, especially when the joke was on her. She relished telling why she had left the Hills. She was cooking in a boarding house and living with a sky pilot who roomed there because the icehouse out back was full of beer. He loved women and beer, in what order Nellie was uncertain until the night of the big fire. Everybody ran like hell for the creek, but the sky pilot kept looking back at the icehouse and tripping over the hem of his nightshirt. Nellie told him to stop that foolishness, he would not listen "—and by god! just when he took his last look, she blew skyhigh and he turned into a pillar of malt!"

She had cooked six years for Milo Smith, when, short-handed for the Saturday night poker game, he ordered her to sit in. Nellie told Badger that she got the hands, bet them, and when the sun came up she went out to cook breakfast in her very own house. She had won eight hundred dollars, a diamond ring, and the entire road ranch situated on a section of deeded land. She ousted Smith and his freeloaders, set the best table between Fort Pierre and Rapid City, and began to enjoy her sunset years. She would have no help but orphan boys. She gave them a clean home, good food, and warm clothes, taught them respect, discipline, and the meaning of honest work; in return, they gave Nellie a measure of devotion that came from love, not fear, and eventually sent each boy out on his own, equipped to tackle anything the world threw at him.

A year and three months ago, Nellie had told Badger that young Lester was not only a fine horse-breaker but showed signs of becoming best of a damned good bunch, would either die young or end up with the biggest ranch in the state. It looked as if Nellie was right again. Lester came running with bedroll and clothes bag, stared gape-mouthed at the spectacle of a grown man puddling calmly around Nellie's kitchen in his wet underwear. Lester was starting to fill out his lanky, long-boned frame, but he still had the wild cowlick in his sandy hair and the crooked nose that started downward toward his incisors and finished aimed at a molar. Big feet and hands, sharp, delft-blue eyes watching Badger closely.

"Lester, can you lay hands on the wash boiler?"

"Huh—sure."

"Washtub, crock, soap, towel?" Thank god, there were no roller towels in Nellie's.

"Yessir!"

Badger lifted the stove lids, helped Lester swing the boiler on, started a new fire while Lester carried water from the porch pump, filled the boiler, set two buckets of cold aside for mixing, brought the washtub and a stone crock from the alcove under the back stairs, found a big yellow towel and soap in the pantry. Badger fed the fire until the surface bubbles broke, peeled off his dirty underwear, filled the tub, added cold to suit his big toe, squatted on the over-turned crock, and enjoyed his first hot bath in ten days. Soaping, he smiled at Lester.

"Paints all right?"

Lester flushed guiltily and tore out of the kitchen to finish his barn chores. Badger rinsed, toweled off, put on clean socks, underwear, and a pair of mocca-sins to wear while his boots dried. He was sitting at the table drinking coffee and eating sugar cookies from Nellie's pussycat bowl when she got rid of her last customer, locked the front door, and trotted down the hall into the kitchen. "Looks like you'll live," she said, and began throwing together a meal for him, "how about some pie, there's half a peach left."

"Sounds good, Nellie."

"Henry, I know why you're here. I got a letter from Mike. No use spouting sad words, you know how I feel. Mike asked me to keep an eye peeled, me and Lester and Birdie ain't let a soul pass unnoticed, but nobody that matches them murdering sonsabitches. I wish you'd go over everything again, and whatever is new."

Badger described the horse-trading outfit while Nellie served his supper, cut the peach pie, sat drinking coffee to keep him company. Eating, Badger said, "What else has happened?"

"Same old round—say, there's gonna be a horse race."

"In November?"

"Good reasons why, Henry. You heard of Pass Johnson?"

"Texas cattleman, got the PJ lease on Cheyenne River Agency."

"That's him. Cattle, fast horses, likes to bet. He brought a thoroughbred racer up last spring, a blaze-faced sorrel that mopped up everything along the river. Out on the Cheyenne, old Jules Babine got hold of a mare that licked all comers. Race is set for Thanksgiving Day on the flats opposite Babine's."

"Babine's mare must be special, to challenge a racer."

"Henry, I think so too. You keep eating, I'll just refresh your memory on those good reasons why."

Nellie reviewed the shape of things along the Cheyenne, which formed the southern boundary of the Cheyenne River Indian Reservation. In 1904 Pass Johnson had leased half a million acres of reservation land to run his Texas steers, with the legal understanding that all mixed-bloods occupying allotments on the reservation be permitted to stay. The larger allotment ranches, run by older mixed-bloods and

squawmen, had their own leases and were no con-
cern, but right from the start the hard-bitten, landless
half-breeds squatting on the south side of the river
were a thorn in Pass Johnson's belly, eating PJ beef
and pushing their cattle and horses north across
the Cheyenne onto PJ leased grass.

Johnson was a man of hard-earned reputation
along the Mexican border. He was also a patient
man who never acted hastily; the half-breeds mistook
his patience for timidity and passed the word that, if
he tried to push their stock south of the river, they'd
kill him. Johnson returned from an extended Texas
trip in October, 1906, called in his men, told them
the story, led them out to cut back the PJ steers and
close-herd the illegal cattle and horses. On the morning of the fourth day of the gather, they had collected
about 300 horses and 2,000 cattle of all sizes, shapes,
and brands. Johnson started the herd for the river
crossing where the half-breeds waited. He rode in
front, rifle at the ready, put the herd across, and rode
back, without a shot fired. A few days later he stated
publicly, in Evarts, that he'd be happy to make a deal
with the devil to spend a few days in hell for permission to kill a dozen of those damned half-breeds and
squawmen. He could name six instantly, but he'd
need a few minutes to pick and choose before he
called off the last half dozen.

He made a lot of people killing-mad. Jules Babine
had two sons and a married daughter living east of
his big place on the south side of the Cheyenne; a
damned Texan had suddenly branded them all
thieves or worse. Babine just happened to be in Le
Beau on the first Sunday in September, in front of
DuFran's saloon, when Johnson rode up. Babine
challenged him to race his sorrel against Babine's
mare on the flats opposite Babine's. Johnson accepted,
they agreed on Thanksgiving Day, bets to go down
before the race, and "——how's that for good reasons
why, Henry?"

"You seen them run?"

"Lester was in Evarts on July fourth. He saw Johnson's sorrel whip a black racer, says he never saw a horse run that fast in his life."

"The mare?"

"Ain't seen her, Henry, but we heard that Babine's worst problem all summer was getting a rider good enough to bring out her best, she's so fast and flighty."

"Who rides?"

"Johnson's got his own man. Sid Hecht stopped by day before yesterday, said Babine was bringing in a real jockey."

"Where do they train, Nellie?"

"The sorrel in Evarts, Babine's mare on his place. Nobody can get near to see her work, much less put a clock on her."

"Nellie, how big is Babine's family?"

"'Bout a dozen children, I think."

"You know any of them, what they do?"

"Met a couple of the older boys, far as I know, all of 'em are home or along the Cheyenne. Sid Hecht knows them."

"Is Sid home?"

"Ought to be—now look here, Henry, you're dead on your feet. Go to bed if you figure on travel tomorrow."

"North, Nellie. Visit Sid, find out if Babine got a rider for his mare."

"Henry, there's times I'm thick-headed as potato soup. I know you're looking for three murdering bastards, but I must of missed a turn back there someplace. I don't connect?"

"You couldn't, Nellie. Remember the one I called Snapper?"

"Sure, you said he was the runt of that outfit."

"He's small enough to be a jockey."

Nellie leaped to her feet, upset the coffeepot, spilled the sugar bowl.

"Great god on the mountain! If this Snapper's a jockey, them other two must be Babine kin."

"Possible, Nellie."

"But why, Henry? Everybody knows Babine's been working this race up for, good christ! at least two years. If Snapper's the jockey, why would they stop and murder your mother—oh hell! I know why. Human beings are capable of anything, no use trying to invent reasons for their actions."

"A dozen children?"

"Which one, eh? Or two, the snakes!"

"Sons, son-in-laws, grandsons—could be any of them, Nellie."

"Henry, I don't need to warn you about being damn careful among them cutthroats."

"I will, Nellie."

"Don't go to thinking you can get one to name the others. They're safe as sin in a church coal bin, ain't no lump dare to call the other black. Maybe I better—"

"No."

"Then how about Lester—?"

"You need him here, Nellie."

"All right, Henry, but come race day, you won't be lonesome for friends. Hell, the whole damn country'll be there!"

Snapper woke to the music of harness creak and saddle-gear clink; the way the team responded to wordless, fingered commands, Brown was on the seat. Snapper slept again, woke in stillness, smelled smoke and coffee on a damp wind.

"Trader?"

"Breakfast stop, Snapper—sleep good?"

"Beats a snoozer berth."

Snapper buttoned up, climbed over the tailgate, found himself the center of attention; half-ghost in fire and darkness, four pairs of eyes under four assorted hatbrims across the coals.

"No time to introduce you now—" Brown handed him a cup, poured coffee "—but the boys are glad to see you."

"Likewise—" Rose gave him a plate of hot biscuits and molasses "—where's Whitey?"

"Up ahead with Flop Ears and the others, they'll get in early."

Snapper ate his breakfast in the fading night become somber dawn as they pulled out. He rode the seat with Brown while sunrise paced their slow climb from the Bad River Valley onto the plateau where clouds ate the sun, put the curse of winter on the land, spat cold rain and sleet that tried to snow as they tipped into the first draws and springheads of the Cheyenne watershed. They followed the closing branches of Plum Creek into the river valley, halted on the south bank where the riders lit and waved three lanterns, got three arcing yellow dots in reply.

"Hang on, Snapper!"

The bay team hit the leather, went down the approach into the river, riders leading and flanking, Rose at drag with the trade string, all bucking the current, hauling the north bank into waving lanterns and welcome whoops that made Snapper think the whole damn Sioux nation had turned out to greet the prodigal son, his daughter, and the skinniest fatted calf a hungry Indian ever saw. They drove through snow-powdered trees around the shoulder of a heavy bluff into a yard backdropped by more trees and the bluff itself. Dogs barked, children yelled, Brown got down and shook hands right and left as he pushed through the crowd to the house, took off his hat and bent his head to the thick, dark shape in the doorway. Behind the canvas flaps, Rose hissed:

"That's Grandpa Babine, you go up there!"

"Kid, you sound scared."

"What for? You go there!"

"Kid, I'll canter when you trot."

Rose swore fiercely, leaped past him into the slush, turned like a cat, waiting. Snapper climbed down and walked beside her to the doorway. Brown said, "Jules, this is him," and the old man's voice rumbled like a capped volcano, "Who wit him?" and Snapper pushed his hatbrim back with one finger and gave Babine look for look.

"A damned good kid, Mister."

For a moment even the dogs were still. Then Babine grabbed Rose, yanked her forward into a bear hug, spun her into the crook of his left arm, and shook Snapper's hand.

"Come!"

Snapper followed them through a houseful of dark faces split in white-toothed grins so filled with friendly greeting that he had a hard time keeping his own jaw set as mean as he wanted to hold it while he was here; on out a back door across the yard into the lantern-lit barn where Babine jerked a hand at two men who led two mouse-colored mares from adjoining box stalls. Babine's cheeks puffed with some inner joke.

"Pick her, Snap."

They expected him to flop, the fish out of water, the bare-butted expert. Snapper said, "Hello, Flop Ears," and walked up to the mare, let her touch his face and shoulders with her muzzle, like a long lost husband returned and welcomed. Rubbing her neck, he lip-murmured so softly the sound did not leave their intimate triangle. The Indian mare edged over gingerly. Snapper let her take a good smell, up and down, clothes, skin, hair, oil; while she judged him, he judged her, using the only comparison that mattered: the thoroughbred mare under his right arm and the picture of the perfect mare in the template of his mind.

Brown had told him how Babine acquired her. She was out of an Appaloosa mare by a part-thoroughbred blood stallion, born near Lapwai and cared for gently until her owner took her across the border into Canada above the Blackfoot Reservation where he brought her to prime without hurry or force, something of a rarity even among dedicated racing men. He raced her five times and won once in her fourth year; in her fifth, the traps baited, she raced five

times and won five times, made her owner the richest mixed-blood in the province of Alberta. He
dropped below the line toward Belle Fourche, making paupers of the stubborn men who insisted that a
whole horse could always beat a mare. Babine sent his
son Jean, and his son-in-law, Dan Bria, to buy the
mare. They brought her home a year ago in October;
come spring, through summer, she beat every fast
runner from Standing Rock to Pine Ridge. She was
the bait in the trap Babine had been nudging toward
Pass Johnson for two years; at the right moment, before a score of witnesses in Le Beau, Johnson took
the challenge.

"What you tink, Snap?"

Snapper walked around the Indian mare, saw how
close, yet how distinctive, the two mares were; knew
where Whitey Crosier would go to work with his
magic brushes, knives, scissors, and combs. He saw
Whitey in the shadows, eyes hidden behind smoked
lenses, mouth showing no emotion. He spoke the
words Babine wanted to hear, "Could be twins, Mister," and saw a wisp of smile touch Whitey's lips.

"Call me Jules."

"When do we start, Jules?"

"You say, Snap."

"Work here mornings, where do we run?"

"Nort."

"Afternoons, same time race will run, we exercise
and run. Whitey, you want any special time?"

"Later, Snapper."

"Gear?"

Brown spoke. "Ready."

Snapper patted the Indian mare. "Hello, Mouse—
who rides Mouse, Trader?"

"Well—"

"Got a scale?"

"Sure."

"Weigh in."

Brown led them to a tack-and-sack room filled with
gear, piles of grain sacks, and a single beam Atlas

platform scale. Snapper added the hundred-pound loose weight to the poise beam rod, ran the marker out to fifteen pounds, and stepped on. The beam rose, stayed, hung dead center when he added one pound.

"Hat, clothes, boots, and bones—hundred and sixteen pounds. Match it or beat it."

Babine said, "We got nobod, Snap."

"Get on, kid."

Rose hung back until Babine motioned. She stepped up and Snapper slid the marker beam back two pounds, three, centered at one hundred and eleven pounds.

"The kid rides."

Babine's mouth formed an angry O.

"Jules, you want to win this race?"

"Hah!"

"I got to know what the mare can do. I can't push her to the limit against a watch. Got to have another horse. We got a good one, we got a jock lighter'n me, that way the kid pushes your mare, your mare pushes Flop Ears."

"You tink Rose so good?"

"Yes."

"You hear, Dan?"

"I hear."

"*Très bien*, take a chance."

Babine marched from the tack room, all followed, one lantern smoked yellowly on the plank floor between Brown and Rose, facing Snapper.

"Trader, don't he like the kid?"

"She's a girl."

"She can ride."

Rose was silent. Brown turned. "Can you do it?"

"If he say so."

"Kid, I say so."

"Then I do it."

Suddenly, without warning, all smiled; a frightening expression of trust by three people who had never trusted. Brown looked at his watch and picked up the lantern.

"Time for bed."

The mares were in their stalls, the night guards were wrapped in buffalo robes on the hay bale stacks. Whitey Crosier had gone, all the people were gone, but not too far, they could be felt in the night. Crossing the yard in the bitter cold, watching Rose turn left toward a separate cabin, following Brown right into a small cabin furnished with an old dresser, washstand, Buckeye wood burner stove, and a neatly made-up army cot, Snapper was silent. Brown struck a match, lit the candle on the washstand, paused at the door.

"All right, Snapper?"

"Trader, what's your square moniker?"

"Dan Bria."

"Better call you Trader, started that way."

"Suits me fine, Snapper."

Brown closed the door, Snapper undressed to his underwear, pinched the candle, got between the blankets. In the morning he had to start proving something that nobody else knew or understood. He could show them what had to be done, to prepare the thoroughbred mare for the race, but he could not tell them if he, years away from tracks and racers, still had the magic in his hands, his legs, the seat of his pants. Maybe he was a has-been and didn't know it; if he was, teaching Rose was more important than even she could guess.

The moment Badger sat down to breakfast, Nellie was after him to rest a few days.

"Your horses need rest."

"I know it."

"Nasty out today, looks like snow."

"Nellie, I got to get up there."

Nellie sighed. "All right, but you're skinny as a rail, for the sake of your belly, I'll fix you a good lunch."

"Me skinny?"

"Lord a mercy, look at you!"

Badger had not looked at himself critically for days. All the fat, the extra weight, had disappeared, he was almost the way he looked at twenty-one, his clothes were hanging on him, his belt was taken up three holes more than where he started. Uncle Bad Knees would not believe his own eyes.

"Nellie, have you got a couple of empty Sunny Brook bottles?"

"Lester?"

Lester ran out the back door. Nellie gathered up Badger's dirty clothes to wash and iron, made a dozen sandwiches, filled a wicker basket with them, hard-boiled eggs, two loaves of bread, and half a ham wrapped in muslin and tinfoil. Lester brought two clean Sunny Brook empties, ran back to the barn, and worked frantically, greasing wagon wheels, oiling harness and moving parts, doing all he could to put the outfit in decent road condition. He muttered, "Watch that rear off wheel," and stood beside Nellie waving goodby as her last words, ripped away on the wind, "Be carefullllll—" saw him off.

Driving north, Badger's impatience was rising; with it, his interest in people was growing, as if his mother's death had forced him out into an alien world and made him pay attention to all the things he used to ignore. Faces, friends, even the killers; all took sharper profile in his thoughts. Was he finally learning to see without using his eyes? Uncle Bad Knees had done that for years.

He did not want to come bursting into the Cheyenne country from the south and make the Babines suspicious. He camped early, got a dawn start, ambled along the east side of Anderson Ridge, crossed Chantier Creek, and angled north by east toward a place where he could rest the paints and do some thinking; next day he threaded on through the spiderweb of spring-fed rivulets and tiny creeks into a stand of heavy timber where Chris Fabre's isolated log cabin stood padlocked. Chris lived in Le Beau most of the time, but during prime fur season had a habit of

wandering off, giving the government fur control
agents the slip, and surfacing in trapping country.
Chris was getting too old for sets in ice water and
snowshoeing through deep drifts, but he still made
two or three short line hauls every winter. Badger
made the blind turn, scratched the wagon through
the last half-mile, drove behind the cabin and sawed
the wagon into a windbreak position on the west side
of the lean-to. He got the paints settled in, dug the
padlock key from its hidey hole, and unlocked the
door. An hour later he was cooking supper in a warming cabin, looking forward to a good night's sleep.

Chris had plenty of canned goods on the shelves,
firewood was stacked head-high against the north
wall; if Badger wanted a change in diet, he could
take a fishline six miles east to the mouth of the
Cheyenne where the Missouri, rushing past, created
a backed-up pool full of fish. Chris had trapped wildcat and lynx in the bottoms, taken mink and beaver
from the creeks upstream; a fox or two was usually
in residence nearby, muskrats were pawing mud and
reed houses in the lagoons, old mossy-horns sometimes
wandered into the thickets and staked permanent
claims. Badger could rest unseen, unheard, with mice
for company, but first he took an empty Sunny Brook
bottle up the path to the blind turn and hung it from
a limb, to warn Chris if he came ghosting through
the night with a pack of illegal pelts. Then Badger
banked the fire, undressed, and got into bed. The
paints needed three days' rest; if Chris had not come
by then, it was time to head west.

Breakfast quieted night's hungry mares. Snapper
ate by himself at the long table in the big house,
served by one of the older women who came and
went wordlessly, left the coffeepot on a block of
wood beside his plate. He wondered if he'd ever
get used to the Indian style coffee with the sugar
boiled in it; he ran to the barn and found a full
house waiting, blowing on clenched fists, stamping

cold feet, peering from turned-up collars at the miracle man. Brown spoke for all:

"How do we start, Snapper?"

"Gear."

They laid it out in neat rows and Snapper warped them into question marks. He examined every strap, stirrup, buckle, ring, rope, whip and bit; shook out every blanket, flexed every bridle, hackamore and halter, went over the saddles from polished seat to pad.

"Blacksmith?"

"Out back, Snapper."

Set snug against the bluff, doors three-quarters closed against weather, inside the annealed odor of iron, fire, oil, smoke, horses, and the smith, a thick-chested grandson called Xavier who started the fire and proved that his bellows pumped, his charcoal burned evenly, his forge heated, his tongs swung the cherry-red iron onto the steel anvil where his hammers beat with authority. He showed Snapper three dozen sets of the special, lightweight racing shoes with five sizes of nails, three sizes of caulks, two new hoof knives, and a large box of medical supplies.

"Good shop, Xavier."

"*Merci*, Snapper."

Back in the barn, Snapper had the mares led out, looked at eight shoes on eight dainty feet, had the young men lead the mares up and down the alleyway while everybody talked and moved around; let them sniff the cat sleeping on the corn sacks, the dog eating a hoof paring stolen from the smithy floor. All shapes, smells and sounds must become familiar to the high-strung ladies.

"Saddle up."

Brown saddled Flop Ears, Rose took Mouse, Snapper felt the once-folded Navajo blankets for humps, thread knots, wrinkles; checked the dangling stirrups, cinches, bridles, motioned for another walk-around, halted them and hooked a finger.

"Get up, kid."

Rose mounted.

"Climb down."

She legged over and slid off. "Why—?"

"Don't waste time, kid. Mount up."

Rose went up, her face dark, her knuckles white on the reins. Snapper moved over to Flop Ears' right side and prepared to mount. When Flop Ears gave outraged protest, Rose understood. Indian horses were mounted on the right side, white horses on the left. Mounting a mare supposed to be Indian on her right side, without previous training, would start a riot.

"Me too, Snapper?"

"You too, kid."

"Will they break?"

"Got to."

"We got time?"

"Take turns so Flop Ears gets used to you, Mouse to me. I want them taking us and all gear with no kiting. We need all the time we can grab to crack the tough nut."

Brown said, "The start?"

"The start, Trader."

The race would be run on the flats across the river, on a straight course laid out from the starting line to a pile of rocks topped by a flag, around that marker and return to the starting line which became the finish. Flop Ears came from a world of supervised starts behind spring lines and out of the new gates coming into vogue onto manicured race tracks flowing past grandstands pulsing with color, band music, and the shouts of orderly thousands cheering a finish run. The flats were prairie sod rooted in the detritus of time, a deceptively smooth surface filled with tiny pebbles, ancient shards, dried up shells and soft rocks ground to gray dust; a surface firm in dry weather and unspeakable in wet. All this could be mastered; but the start?

Walk-up, two horses approached the starter sitting his horse, right arm raised, holding his revolver

at full cock. If satisfied both horses were even, the
starter pulled trigger, the shot sent them away.
Flop Ears was not gunshy but she was not trained to
beat the gun. Nor was Mouse trained to do the trick.
Snapper explained how he wanted to teach both
mares to watch the hammer on the starter's revolver;
as it fell, he wanted them to jump out, beat the shot
sound by a split second. It meant nothing in terms
of distance, but the mare would be off and running
before the sorrel moved. Standing between the mares,
Rose asked the expected question:

"How come they see the hammer fall?"

"Sharp eyes, kid."

"How you make 'em do it?"

"Work and sweat."

"Practice?"

"Makes perfect, kid."

"Better—this Flop Ears, she's dumb."

"Mouse's smart?"

"Smarter. Ain't sayin' much."

"Kid, you're saying Mouse learns first?"

"Yes."

"Whitey, what do you say?"

"Miss Rose may have a point, Snapper. Mouse has
a good head, sharp eyes. I like the way she moves."

Whitey Crosier was saying, in a language spoken
by himself and Snapper, that Mouse was odds-on to
have more brains, but brains in the case of horses
was adding one grain of sand to a beach. You rarely
had the exquisite sense of weight necessary to tell
the difference.

"Trader, you got the right gun?"

"Same make as the starter's, same caliber and car-
tridges."

"Blanks?"

Somebody snorted. Brown said, "We don't use
blanks out here, Snapper."

"Good, the starter can shoot the loser for dog meat."

7

On the second night a raccoon tried to sneak under the tarp into the wagon box, but the paints let Badger know and his lantern reflector caught the masked bandit red-handed. Badger said, "Don't run, Brother," and put a pie tin of canned milk at the lean-to corner. He rose early on the third morning, locked the door, hid the key, jerked the Sunny Brook bottle off the string as he passed beneath the limb. He drove an old game trail along the north flank of Cedar Butte, wound through the low range of hills called the Crockett Mountains, dropped into the Sansarc Creek Valley. Sid Hecht was waiting at the corner of a new barn, rifle ready to welcome friend or foe.

"Henry, by god! Nellie said you might show—pull under that shed."

Badger drove the wagon under the machine shed roof, led the paints to the corral behind the barn, pumped water into the trough Sid had hollowed out of a big cedar log five years ago. Walking toward the house, he shaded his eyes to see clearly.

"Sid, when did you get done?"

"Last spring. House is ten by twenty, notched logs, half-log floor, tarpaper under the shingles. Go on in, Henry."

Sid stopped to cut their supper off the hind quarter of O.P. beef. Badger went inside, dropped his gear, admired the meld of old and new: brass bed,

cookstove, and copper pots from the old shack; new
round oak table and six chairs, blue willow dishes,
hard coal base-burner, and a red and black rag rug.
When Sid came in with two steaks, Badger pointed
to the rug.

"Whose apple you polish?"

"Marge Lee made it herself."

"Are you——?"

"Not by a damn sight, not yet!" Sid set out two
glasses, a bottle of Overholt, and a fruit jar of spring
water from the coulee west of the house. He poured
and lifted his glass. "Nellie told me about your Ma.
Let's drink to finding them sonsabitches!"

"Thanks, Sid."

"How's your uncle, rest of the family?"

"Fine, last time I saw them. You been all right?"

"Run of good luck, Henry."

"I saw your hay."

"Tops thirty ton, all stacked and fenced. Got
some good colts this year."

Sid cooked supper with speed and ease, little
changed from the day they met in 1893. Badger and
his uncle were on the road south from Fort Bennett,
overhauling a man limping under saddle and bedroll. Uncle Bad Knees said, "Get in," and Sid swung
his gear, used one hand as a fulcrum, jumped over
the sideboard into the box. Coal black hair, eyes
blacker in his long, bony face. Sid looked big until
you got to know him and realized that he was average
height; but rock-solid through the chest and arms,
giving off the feeling that he could walk straight
through trouble. On that dusty, long-ago spring day,
young Henry Badger turned on the wagon seat and
offered the canteen. Sid drank, sloshed, drank again,
told them how his horse had died off west, with him
due in Fort Pierre next day to join a roundup crew.
Uncle Bad Knees said, "We get you there," and Sid
took a longer drink, returned the canteen, and sighed
happily.

Rattling along that day, through the night, young

Sid Hecht told them how he rode the Burlington west from Omaha to Siding Seven, worked one day on that lousy end-of-track job, hiked north through the Hills to Rapid City, bought a ticket to Buffalo Gap, walked over to Hot Springs, and toted brick for a mason at $2.25 a day while paying $4.50 a week to a boarding house. Eight days later he hired on to help drive three hundred horses to Fort Pierre, liked the river country and squatted near the mouth of Plum Creek, across from the Cherry Creek subagency. Raising cattle was chancy for a kid, but Sid did odd jobs, met people, got wise in due time and turned to horses. Uncle Bad Knees' name hadn't meant a thing to Sid on first meeting, but later, when he got to separating lions from lambs, he told Henry Badger that the day he mentioned Uncle Bad Knees to Circle Lame, the old Sioux trembled like a fall leaf in a high wind. It took Sid the better part of a day and night to pry the story of the swift runner and his vengeance on the Sioux out of the old chief and his nephews. In passing time Sid got to know Hump, Little Bear, Dupre, Narcelle, Babine, Rousseau, all the old-timers who knew the country well. Sid stayed on, helped make it worth living in, showed what sweat and guts could do; from a green Iowa boy of eighteen to the best horse rancher along the river at forty, was proof aplenty of Sid's ability and courage.

"Big race still on, Sid?"

"Hot as ever."

"Babine get his jockey?"

"That's what I heard—but how about you, anything new since I saw Nellie?"

"The same three Nellie told you about, Sid."

Sid turned the steaks, slid the pan of biscuits into the warming oven.

"You ain't up here for your health, Henry. What the hell they headed north for?"

"They're tied into the horse race."

Sid turned in surprise. "Tied in with Jules Babine? That old man don't stand for murder."

"That's what I think, Sid. Not him, but he's got a
big family. Can you name them, tell me what they
do?"

"Jules' wife is dead. Amadee, Ambrose and Isabelle
are dead. Bill's home. Sarah married Manuel Gra-
velle, they live up on the Cannonball. Fred's home,
Annie married Tom LeBrun, he's dead, she's home,
her oldest boy Xavier is the best blacksmith around
here. Jean's home. Isabelle married Dan Bria, he's
from somewhere above Fort Yates. They had one
kid, a girl, before Isabelle was drowned in that
flood two years after I got here. Dan lives at home.
Helen married Napoleon Jolliffe, they live on this
side of the river, across from the mouth of Fishgut
Creek. Narcisse and Charley live on down from
them. Home or downriver, they're all in the cattle
and horse business."

"Any of them travel?"

"Jean makes the business trips for old Jules. He's
good with horses, but Dan Bria is better. Jules sent
them out to Belle Fourche last year to buy the racing
mare. Summers, Dan takes an outfit east, makes all
them little county fairs and race meets, buys, sells,
trades horses. They call him Trader."

"What kind of outfit, Sid?"

"Big camp wagon, good team, string of trading
stock."

"How about the grandsons?"

"Oh jesus! there must be thirty, and that many
girls too. Home, gone, married, dead. I can't keep
track—Henry, what's wrong?"

"Sid, you named him."

"Oh my god! You sure?"

"Pour another drink, Sid. I'll tell you the hind end
of a horse-race story, then you tell me if I'm wrong."

Whitey Crosier played starter, sitting an old high-
hipped, plop-footed hiderack turned out to pasture
and the children. Flop Ears tended to wince at shot
sound, so Snapper began teaching her to jump when

his knees clamped a certain way. Walking toward the line scratched in the dirt between Whitey and Brown, head held straight, Flop Ears could see the revolver in Whitey's right hand but could not see his left hand signal the tipoff to Snapper as his trigger finger squeezed and the hammer fell; but Flop Ears had to learn that hammer fall and knee clamp meant jump just before the shot sounded. Mouse was breaking equally fast to the same sequence, left eye watching Whitey's gun hand, responding instantly to Rose's clamped legs. It seemed to Snapper that Mouse was learning the trick more rapidly by eye than Flop Ears was by knee.

They practiced the start, exercised, ran the course marked by two plow furrows and a pile of rocks; changed mares and repeated the run. Each day warmed more slowly, each workout had a sharper bite of urgency, saw Babine lose more of his fear that Rose would come a cropper. At each day's end Snapper led his troop down the creek trail into the yard where, since the first workout, he had dismounted and tossed his reins to the young men with the same words, "Where's the hot-walkers?" and followed the others into the tack room where they argued like a bunch of shyster lawyers over the day's progress and loss. After that it was wash, eat and relax.

Babine played muggins, drank wild grape wine, and talked. He bit off his words, called Snapper "Snap," made "fiddle" come out "fid," turned "the" into "de," spoke two distinct words for "sona bitch." The women and unmarried girls gathered at the far end of the big room but Rose sat behind Babine with the children, kept her mouth tight-shut, listened to the horse talk. One night blended into another, Snapper learned strange, wild, crazy, unbelievable things: calf meat was too rich for white men, gave them belly cramps; if you didn't own a pair of hard-toed boots, it was better to be a wallflower at local dances; if your dogs chased cattle, you shot them; never bait carcasses with strychnine on the reservation, it was

against the law; raw liver from a young antelope
with some of the gall squeezed on it, tasted better
that way than just plain; stay out of Evarts on Satur-
days and July 4th; don't wear a gun into DuFran's
saloon in Le Beau; all tribal medicines were different, each tribe had its own carefully guarded doses
and charms. The Blackfoot used sagebrush heads
for heartburn and mountain fever; the Sioux blew
powdered Clementis root up a horse's nose to stimu-
late it; the Nez Percé chewed up wild peony root,
made a horse swallow it, to give him long wind and
great desire to win. Pawnees boiled the tops and
leaves of sticky herbs, washed galls and sores in the
solution. Xavier had discovered nine cures for worms.
Whitey Crosier gave Xavier a tenth practiced far to
the south, tulip tree bark pounded into powder. While
he talked, Whitey kept carving a figure from a wood
block with his sharp knife; that night he finished
a frog with bulging eyes and asked Rose to pass it to
the little girl with the big brown eyes. She whispered in Rose's ear. Rose said,

"Go on, Mary."

Mary thanked Whitey. He smiled and bowed his
head. Mary whispered to Rose who spoke again,
"Mary asks what are you?"

"Cajun."

"What's that?"

"Cajuns are those of French-Acadian ancestry who
live in the Bayou Teche parish of Louisiana. Long,
long ago our ancestors came from Acadia, now called
Nova Scotia."

Xavier's son Baptiste said, "Why you white, eh?"

"You know the white *letiche,* the ghost of the child
who died unchristened, doomed to haunt unseen the
bedrooms of children?"

"No."

"You know the goblin that milks cows and shears
sheep?"

"No."

"You know the *loup-garou?*"

"Oui!"

"You believe in four-leaf clovers and lucky horse-shoes?"

"You bet!"

"Will a spider in a nutshell cure fever?"

"I don't know."

"All these very valuable things you don' know? Tsk, tsk! Then you won' know why I'm white if I tell you."

"Why you white?"

"I fell in a paint bucket."

"When?"

"How old are you, Baptiste?"

"Nine."

"Then I was nine."

Babine swallowed his smile behind his roar, "To bed wit you!" and the women shooed the children away, brought more wine, scurried back to the far end of the room. Hens, Snapper thought, nice fat hens with their good-looking spring fryers, and what sat beside him in the same clothes she wore all day riding mares? The female weasel in the henhouse. Then Xavier asked Whitey if it was difficult to disguise a horse, and Snapper realized they had waited a long time to ask that question. Whitey put his knife away and nodded gravely.

"Xavier, you understand the ringer?"

"Yes, but tell it, please."

"Start with a selling race," Whitey said. "An owner enters his horse in such a race with the agreement to sell the horse at a specified price. You find a fast horse that looks like another horse you have spotted, one with a terrible record because he is so slow. You buy this slow horse. You enter the slow horse in the last race of the last day of a meet at some far-off park, where all the judges will be running to catch the train to the next track. You make the switch, bring in the fast horse, doctor him to look exactly like the slow horse, he goes to the post at long odds. Before the odds can change in far-off cities—where your people place the bets, you never bet at the track or in the nearby city—the race is over, your ringer has won, the bookmakers must pay off."

"Are you good at it, Whitey?"

"Xavier, I am one of the best with the tools— dyes, paints, powders, chalks, hair, the art of changing one horse into another. But not at setting up such races."

"Who does that, Whitey?"

"I worked for the best man once, Xavier. His name is Chilson, the Pinkertons and newspaper reporters called him King of the Ringers. I did jobs for him at Fair Grounds and Gravesend. He pulled off the biggest coup of all time on October 3rd, 1903, in the closing race at Morris Park. He entered a horse called Fiddler. His associates placed bets across the country from Boston to San Francisco. Fiddler won the race, the total take topped three million."

Babine said, "Is true, Blanc?"

"Yes, Jules."

"You fix de horse?"

"Yes."

"Sona bitch!" Babine said admiringly. "That Fid, he some horse, eh?"

"The horse that ran was some horse—" Whitey smiled at Xavier "—you have talked about horse medicine. I have watched it work in the Nations. How goes it here, to win or lose?"

Xavier told how cottonwood bark rubbed on a horse made him brave, how Blackfoot made a little rawhide horse and painted a small rock with their secret medicine. When your horse ran against another, the rawhide horse became the other. If you wanted it to fly the track, you put the rock on the rawhide head. Want it to buck, on the shoulders. Want it to kick up, on the hind legs. Another good one was rubbing a willow stick with secret medicine. Your jockey carried this stick in the race, could reach over and touch the other horse, make it fall back. If the other horse gained, drop the stick in its tracks, it would

surely falter. Xavier spoke of famous Indian racers:
Wind, the original Mouse, old White Eye, and a great
horse simply named Racer. He turned innocently to
Snapper and said:

"What would you do, you see a horse wringing its
tail?"

"Shoot the owner."

"Ah," Xavier said, and all echoed, "Ah! Good,
good!"

Babine said, "How she go, Snap?"

"Good, good!"

Everybody laughed, Babine loudest of all. He gave
Snapper a pat on the shoulder and rose for bed.

"You do it all now, Snap?"

"Everything but monkey drill, Jules."

The last thing Sid said before he slept was, "Henry, you ain't wrong," and the first thing Badger heard
when he woke was, "Henry, I slept on it and you're
still right. Bria's your man."

"But who's the third one?"

"I got no idea."

"Should I bell the cat, Sid?"

"No use, Henry. Babine won't let anybody go till
the race is run. Don't worry, they ain't going nowhere."

Sid did not dislike Pass Johnson personally, but he
got a bellyful of cattle-company manners during his
early years along the Cheyenne. When the big outfits
went on roundup, they kept all the odd brands in a
day herd called the cut, and because many little
ranchers could not afford to follow along to the finish
divvy, a lot of those strays were shipped to Chicago
and the sale money put in the stray account. Sid had
never heard of a little rancher getting paid for lost
steers. Once he was in Chicago and went to see the
Stock Association rep, and the rep told him he'd have
to bring a lawsuit to get his money. Sid told the rep
that he'd collect on the range any way he could.

Sid reckoned that the Stock Association lost more than it gained over the years; no wonder he wanted to see that race on Thanksgiving Day.

"Besides," Sid added, "your team needs rest and new shoes, and your wagon can stand a going-over."

"I know it, Sid. Then I'd like to take a closer look."

"Why not? Go up the river—got a pair of glasses?"

"Yes."

"Find a good place to squat on one of those ridges, where you can look down across the flats all the way to Babine's."

"I could scout until the race, Sid."

Sid looked at the calendar. "Leave the time open. I'll look for you by supper on the twenty-fourth. If you ain't back by morning, I'll come looking."

Snapper wondered if anyone could read his mind. The doubt began on the day he stepped up the pace, ran the full distance at speed. Rose held Mouse on his right stirrup, increased or checked her pace to match his as they ran the course. They changed mares and went through the routine of mounting opposite to natural habit, switched spots, and walked up, Mouse on the imaginary rail nearest the starter's revolver; and so it went as the days passed. Walk-up, hammer falling, jump out, shot sound, running on the grass, Flop Ears in the lead, Mouse clinging like a burr, around the rock pile and back to the finish line. Snapper made minute changes in stirrup position, tied and retied reins, shook the saddles to watch the cinches move; all the while waiting for his old feeling to return. He was in tiptop shape, legs strong, hands limber, eyes clear, seat as perfect as a man ever assumed that unnatural position; and he felt nothing.

His seventh sense was gone. The feeling that tingled in the fingertips and seat, rose through the fingers and hips into the arms and body, met near the lungs and entered the head, made him feel that nobody could beat him if the horse would respond. In the old days it was a thing of wonder to him that a man could transmit desire to a horse, feel the horse lift, become a part of the man's hands and legs as the man welded himself to the horse for that last run, that surge of flying through and beyond normal capabilities, into the stretch, the wire, standing on the turn, slowing, turning, meeting the mascot pony on the way to the winner's circle. He could no more describe what had taken place than he could open up his head and let somebody count the wrinkles in his brain. But it was there and, for a long time, he rarely threw a race when he was on a horse of that caliber.

Now, on the prairie in the middle of nowhere, he sat a truly fine mare and was afraid to say, "Go all out!" because Rose would push him, and if he could not lift the mare, she would not respond, give him that needed extra, he had to bring that much to her to take that much from her on Thanksgiving Day. Whitey Crosier had watched the Johnson sorrel run twice during the summer and come away with healthy respect for a fast horse, but reassured that Flop Ears, ridden by someone with Snapper's magic, could whip the sorrel at all distances up to and including two miles. On the coldest day thus far, ice on the creeks and river, frost on the grass, they rode north to the course; and it was time, even the mares were expectant, ears twitching, eyes rolling in their whites.

"Today's the day, kid. Go all out."

That was the way to catch a young jockey, make him act instinctively, give him no time to think and sweat; or was it for the benefit of the old jockey who tried to sweat and felt like an empty dustbin. Whitey's trigger finger squeezed, the hammer fell, both mares broke like quail, out and off, scattering frost behind them in a thousand broken crystals. Across the flat toward the rock pile, Flop Ears held the lead, ran beautifully under taut control. Around the rock pile, running smoothly, Snapper called on her with his hands, his legs, willed his urgency into her, kept the whip in his teeth, if he could not bring her home with hands and legs, he was done and the mare would know it. He heard Mouse on his left, Rose had cut her corner close, grabbed the inside, she was talking to Mouse, he knew she was far up and low on Mouse's neck, lips pulled back from those small, sharp teeth, callused hands gripping the reins so tightly Mouse had no error margin, had to run as Rose willed; now he heard her swearing in Sioux, in god alone knew what other savage tongues, blistering the hide off Mouse. Rose could lift that Indian mare, he felt it in her, it made him try again, and this time something went from him into Flop Ears; she stretched and began running the way she could, the way Whitey had described her stride when he told where she was bred, born, weaned, babied, trained, and taught—to what finish! A line scratched in frozen dirt! They flashed between Brown and Whitey, so close it was almost a dead heat, eased up and turned, the mares walked side by side, good friends ready for more.

"How close, kid?"

"Neck."

"You go all out?"

"Sure, you said to."

"You pushed her, she needs it."

Brown called, "Any more today?" and Snapper signaled no, they rode for home in the fading light, arrived in full darkness, by silent assent did not meet in the tack room, went their separate ways to wash for supper. Snapper trotted to his cabin, took off his shirt, dropped his underwear over his belt, soaped and scrubbed and rinsed, dried off; was buttoning a clean shirt when the knock sounded.

"Come in!"

Whitey entered, ducked to miss the lintel, closed the door and removed his hat.

"What's up, Whitey?"

"Snapper, Mouse is a good mare, Rose is a fine jockey."

"No arguments here."

"So how come you win by one neck? Flop Ears can beat Mouse easy. You and me—we know that. I think Rose knows it now, perhaps Trader guessed too. Were you holding back today?"

"A little, Whitey. Being careful on that ground."

Whitey shook his head. "She has never stumbled in six years. Tomorrow you let her run like she can, or I will think—"

"What?"

"Snapper, I don' know. Do you?"

Snapper buttoned his shirt, thumbed up his suspenders, put on his sheepskin coat.

"What if I know, Whitey?"

"Then we got big trouble, man. I contract to win this race for Jules Babine. Last spring when Jean came seeking me out, I say, 'Jean, I got a fast mare, you got a fast mare, from these pictures I can make mine look like yours. Get us a good jockey to bring out the best in my mare, give me a look at the other man's horse, and I'll tell you if we win or lose.' That's how she goes, Snapper. I came north, I watched the sorrel, I knew my mare could win with a good jockey. Then Trader tells Jean of you, I came and looked, and *sacre bleu!* it was you, oh man, I told them you were a great jockey in your time, you could win on my mare, and here you are, but are you the great jockey now? Don' lie to me. You and me, we know how it comes and goes."

Snapper could not lie to a man who laid all his cards out face up.

"Whitey, I lost it."

"Oh goddamn! I feared so!"

"Let me try tomorrow."

"Just to see?"

"One more time, to make sure."

"One time more, Snapper. If you don' get it back, then what?"

"Whitey, keep your lip buttoned. I know what to do."

"By god! I'm happy somebody knows."

They walked to supper, ate, sat listening to the talk, watching the muggins game, each ready to help the other if somebody raised a doubt; but nobody was worried, the fools believed that Mouse was that fast! Snapper excused himself early, went to the cabin, sat in bed most of the night, hugging his knees, feeling his drawn-up legs under his fingers, knees lumpy with old knots and scars, calf muscles stringy and lean, right anklebone twice normal size, ever since St. Louis twelve years ago, what were the actors in those costume plays always yelling? The king is dead, long live the king! He slept on that, woke early, ate early, one small man in a big room, bent over plate and cup, gone before others filled the room with bulk and sound; across the wind-swept yard into the barn, quick look at the mares, quicker look at steps behind.

"Early for you, kid."

"Can't sleep."

"You ain't lonesome."

"Bad day."

"Sure as hell is!"

"Wind up, better run now, don't wait for afternoon."

"Kid, you're the weatherman."

They saddled the mares, waited on the others, rode against the wind on a bitter day; warmup was brief, they walked-up before Snapper had time to collect reins and thoughts, gather himself, take Flop Ears off to her best start to date, a sudden uncoiling lump that put her a half-length out front and kept her there to the rock pile; coming around, heading for home, trying to lift her, he had nothing, all he lifted was the weight of memory that covered him with leaden grace. Rose was at his stirrup, his shoulder, neck, cursing Mouse, Snapper did not lift Flop Ears, the wild, foul-mouthed girl and the Indian mare had so much to spare that Flop Ears stole some and crossed the line a neck in front. No, only a head, Rose told him when they turned, then:

"You all right?"

"Sure, kid."

Brown gave him an odd look and shivered. The wind was gusty, anything could happen to a rider. Whitey called, "Let's go in!" and they rode south, collars raised against the chasing wind, left the horses at the barn and went their private ways. Snapper closed his cabin door and sat on the cot; his arms felt dead, his fingers trembled. He had no time to wash, calm down, before the knock came.

"Come in!"

Expecting Whitey, he was not ready for Brown and Rose. Whitey closed the door, all three faced him. Whitey spoke:

"One short neck, Snapper."

"Plenty on this lousy day!"

"Last night you told me, 'Whitey, keep your lip buttoned, I know what to do.' I never said a word at the barn, Snapper. Trader and Rose came to me. They want to help, but you've got to tell us: is it gone?"

"I lost it," Snapper said. "The kid knows it today. When did you read my palm, Trader?"

"Today, Snapper. Like Whitey says, what can we do? We got to win this race."

"No time to fool," Whitey said. "Whatever you got in mind, we better do it in a week or start running now."

Snapper stood and walked to the window, turned with the idea taking shape in his mind, his eyes, in his curled, aching fingers.

"Will you listen to me? Goddam it! I mean, *listen!*"

"Yes, Snapper."

"Kid, I know you will. But they got to put their stamp on it, and then you got to see Babine."

Brown said, "Tell us, Snapper."

Snapper said, "I can't tell it twice. I try that, I lose my own nerve. To start: I ride Flop Ears, we lose the race. Mouse can't beat the sorrel, we know that. But the kid up on Flop Ears, you got another horse race—no, shut up, Trader! Don't say nothin', let me unwind. Flop Ears, the kid up, can lick that sorrel, but not just walking up to the gun on Turkey Day and running around the course. This man Pass Johnson, he knows Jules got a jockey: me! So they look for me, and they plan that way. Johnson's man is bound to be good, he knows his horse, he'll give me a run for my money. But what happens when the kid comes out on Flop Ears, remember, Flop Ears rung in for Mouse by Whitey. I'll tell you what happens. They look for me, what happened, they say? what goes on? When you start asking questions, that spells trouble, they start doubting everything in the race. They look at the kid, and they look at the mare! Listen, Whitey can run a ringer under anybody's nose because he uses the same old con every time: people see what they expect to see. Now listen!

"Can Jules get word to Pass Johnson by somebody Johnson believes, sneak the word to him by Tuesday night that old Jules Babine is working the ringer game, that the jockey—me—will ride up to that starting line on Babine's mare Mouse, but if they're smart, they'll take a damn good look at the Mouse because she ain't, she's a flop-eared running jessie from New Orleans. All right, say Johnson gets the word, he's the kind of man won't say anything until all the bets are down and his man on that sorrel, and me on the Mouse, are ready to start. That's when he springs it, and goes for the marks everybody out here knows— the white stockings on Mouse's forelegs. He'll rub 'em, and off comes whatever it is on his hands, and the solid color shows through, meaning that a ringer is running for the Indian mare.

"Right there, Babine has to do the toughest job of all. He's got to cuss, and raise hell, and say all right you sona bitches! we race you, by god! we race you, and he yells and I ride the ringer off, and the kid here is led through the crowd by Trader on the real Mouse, everybody can see that, and old Jules has got to get them started right then, tell the starter to go, and once they're off, a race is a race. Trader, your people got to be all around that course to keep anybody from spookin' the mare with the kid up, make damn sure she gets a clean run. When she goes round that rock pile and heads for home, don't let nobody out on that course. Kid, when you cross the line, keep on going through the crowd for the river. Trader, you and Jean got to be ready, with plenty of people to cover, get across that river into the barn. Babine's people got to grab all those bets and run. I'll be hitting the water with the ringer first off the bat. Everything's got to go bang-bang-bang! Don't give 'em no time to think after they expose the ringer.

"Sure, you say, Snapper's gone crazy! Mouse can't beat that sorrel with the kid up. Well, the kid ain't riding Mouse, she's on Flop Ears. Whitey, winter coats are getting nice and ragged, make for good trimming. Can you take Flop Ears and Mouse, change them around, then take the Flop Ears ringer and ring her right back to be the Mouse, so Johnson can rub off whatever you cover those white stockings with, and see the solid color legs that won't rub off. Can you change Mouse into Flop Ears, and then work Flop Ears into the Mouse, so Johnson exposes the chance, get everybody looking at me riding that ringer underneath, all the colors solid so nothin' rubs off? Then the kid comes in on a ringer Mouse, Flop Ears under, and runs the race on a ringer running for a ringer. She can win it, Trader. Give her the chance, get everybody looking at me riding that ringer off, start the race, and the kid can do it. Don't say nothin' yet. I'm gonna ask Whitey one question: Can you pull it off?"

"Yes!"

"Trader, can Jules hold up his end?"

"Yes!"

"Kid, I ain't asking you nothin'. You ride!"

"Yes, Snapper!"

"Now get outa here! Don't come back unless you mean business."

Sid loaned Badger his blue-roan roper, a close-built, short-backed horse with black legs and head. A friend of Sid's named Two Bears who lived on Little Moreau Creek traded a pack of beaver for the horse and rode him down to repay Sid a big favor done five years earlier. Sid named the horse after his bowlegged uncle in Iowa. Uncle Oscar had a good disposition, was strong and wiry, and never sulked; neither did his namesake. Oscar knew his business so well that the roper on him better not miss his catch because Oscar went to the fire no matter what. Badger rode him between horseshoeing sessions and wagon overhaul; on the fourth morning Sid saw him off.

"You be back on time, Henry. I ain't missing that race!"

Badger sent Oscar ambling down Sansarc Creek to the river, took the south bank road past mixed-blood cabins, homesteader shacks, and odder chips of flotsam beached by fate or lack of funds. He turned up Hermaphrodite Creek, returned a young mixed-blood's wave, met his wife, drank fresh coffee with plenty of sugar. He heard a child breathing thickly in the rocker box behind the stove and tapped his chest; the woman nodded glumly. Badger said, "Wait," and ran out to his possible sack, brought a ready-to-mix mustard plaster, showed her how to prepare it, guided her hands as he smoothed it on the child's chest, told

119

her to loosen it every hour and listen close for sounds of thinning congestion. She was wary until he spoke Brulé.

"Trust me, sister."

She clapped her mouth. "You speak my tongue!"

"Talk 'em all, sister. Brulé, Oglala, even those cheapskates up north."

Her husband grinned at the old joke about the Miniconjous. "Where you goin'?"

"Home, then I heard about the race. Can the mare beat a whole horse?"

"Everybody says so."

"I got to see it—listen, can I camp up this creek?"

"Old dugout, two, three mile."

"Thanks. I'll stop back, see how the little princess is."

Riding, he wondered if the man was one of those who sat a horse the day Pass Johnson drove the herd across the river. He spotted the dugout, hide-and-pole door dangling on one thong; the roof solid, the inside reasonably dirty, camping on Hermaphrodite Creek without fighting off rattlesnakes was a pleasure. He tied the door in place, cooked and ate supper, tried to sleep and failed; fixed a big lunch and rode down across the creek and up the west slope in full darkness. Oscar topped the ridge and descended carefully into the next creek valley, ascended to the ridgetop plateau. Badger dismounted on the west edge in a fringe of brush and waited on sunrise. boots crushing the light frost on the grass; focused his binoculars with the first sunlight, swept the broad flats below, the course of the river, the smoke from Babine chimneys rising under the bluff. He caught the glint of sunshine on metal, saw the brass tube in a tree fork on the south bank of the river. He sank cross-legged to the cold earth, worked his elbows inside his knees, hunched forward in a tight, dark knot; reins over his right arm, watching the brass tube, he waited. When a few clouds passed beneath the sun, Badger ran, pulling Oscar from the edge of the ridge, changing his plan to fit circumstances. He rode his own back-trail down Hermaphrodite Creek, stopped at the cabin, found the child breathing freely. The woman boiled fresh coffee, served Badger and her husband, stood politely in the corner with the child in her arms, fingering the soft baby hair, smiling at the mustard-seed man. Badger grinned.

"Worked, eh?"

"Yes."

Her husband said, "Dugout too dirty?"

"Not bad, but my friend's house is better."

"Sid Hecht."

"You know him?"

"Sure, he's a good man. You got his roping horse there."

Badger rose and buttoned his coat. They came outside to say goodby, watched him mount and touch his hat. The woman's eyes shone with childhood recollection: along the White? Certainly in the Rosebud. She spoke in Brulé:

"What do they call you?"

"Iruka."

He saw her face as he rode. Not yet twenty, but old enough to remember the stories, perhaps she had seen him long ago on Bull Creek, or passing the Episcopal Mission. She would tell her husband, would he tell Babine that Iruka had come to see the race? If he did, Snapper and Bria had to hear the same news. He said, "Go home, Oscar," and Oscar sailed along the river road, up Sansarc Creek, into the barn corral an hour before sunset. Sid came from the house in his underwear and moccasins; listened to the story and haw-hawed all the way back to the house over what a danged fool a man could be when he let imagination trample common sense.

"You're right, Sid. Babine won't let anybody in until that race is run. And nobody out either."

"Telescope?"

"Pretty sure."

"Make out the man?"

"Not clear, but he looked big."

"On a guess, Fred LeBrun."

"Something else—" Badger described the mixed-blood, his Brulé wife, their child, how he deliberately gave his Brulé name to the woman as he left. Sid nodded.

"That's Little Joe Mulot."

"Will he tell Babine?"

"Sure, Little Joe and Charley Babine are good friends, go partners on most deals along with Narcisse Babine. Don't worry, I get along fine with them."

"Then we wait."

"On the twenty-fifth we'll take your team and wagon, Henry, and head for the flats. Make camp, watch the fun—weather permitting. It's too damned warm for November."

"Sid, Thanksgiving Day will be cold and clear. Every medicine man from Fort Yates to Pine Ridge is casting bones. You want to buck *them?*"

The temperature started dropping on Monday; high for the day by Sid's thermometer was 58 degrees, warm enough to turn the light snowfall into rain. Colder on Tuesday, with only a trace of moisture. That night Sid brought Oscar inside the barn with the paints. The wagon looked good as new but Sid found a hairline crack in the right front tire that could fracture over a bad bump. There was nothing Badger could do about that but try to dodge the rocks. They rose early and got away at sunrise, Sid on Oscar, Badger on the wagon seat, down the creek, west along the river road under a wet, gray sky on a day steadily growing colder. By the time they crossed Hermaphrodite Creek, they had become an unwilling part of a landrush crowd. Wagons rolled ahead and behind, riders passed in duos, trios, and choruses; buggies bounced along, across the river Badger saw long lines of Indian ponies snaking over the ridges toward the river crossings. The Sioux were coming from Cheyenne River Agency, Standing Rock Agency, Rosebud, Pine Ridge, Lower Brulé, everywhere in the country. By the time Sid led the way up the slope into camp on the middle fork ridge, they could see people pouring in from every direction. Sid called hello to a dozen, touched his hat to more, pointed out how the camp areas were forming: Indians along the north bank of the river, teams unharnessed, tents up, smoke rising from cookfires; in the bottom between east and middle fork, all the ranch roundup and supply wagons; nearby were two wagon saloons with drop shutter sides facing the race course, and a quick-lunch wagon selling sandwiches, beans and coffee; higher up the east fork, tents pitched in the middle of a circle of sixteen assorted half-platform and three-seater wagons, were the members of an entire excursion train special from Huron; along all the creeks, on the flats, more people from Pierre, Chamberlin, Rapid City, Yankton, Mitchell, Sioux Falls, Devil's Lake. Badger saw a skinny fellow on a bay horse coming down the fork from the top ridge and called:

"Lester!"

Lester waved, galloped back up the ridge, returned leading a light handy wagon pulled by matched buckskins, driven by a red-haired woman whose open mouth formed words before she reached roaring distance. She and Lester had left the road ranch yesterday, "Just followed the crowd," and if nobody objected, she'd take over the kitchen. Lester unhitched the buckskins, put them and his bay with the other horses, unloaded dutch ovens, groceries, and grub boxes from the handy wagon. Badger fed grain to all the horses while Sid carried wood and Nellie cooked supper. They ate in the shelter of the pitched tarps, a pair of reflector lanterns making the night feel warmer than it was. Nellie loaded her dutch ovens for breakfast and joined them facing the fire Sid had built against a log. Sid talked a few minutes, tossed his cigar into the fire, and rose.

"I'll gad a little."

Lester poked the log and rubbed his nose; a big

soot spot on his right cheek made him look like a
pirate. Nellie pulled off her overshoes, rubbed her
feet in their thick, fuzzy German socks, waved at the
dots of light on the flats below.

"Where's the race course, Henry?"

Badger pointed, Nellie sighted along his arm. "See
that big fire there—?"

"Got it."

"West of the starting line. They'll run east to a pile
of rocks, go around, and come back."

"Where's the betting ground?"

"Between the starting line and the river."

"Any action?"

"Not yet. Sid says it'll all happen in a hurry tomorrow."

Nellie lowered her voice. "All right—any luck?"

Badger told her everything he had learned. Nellie
agreed with Sid, "—watch the race, get a good look
at Snapper and Bria, then make your move. What'll
they do then?"

"Nellie, I can't see Snapper staying. They've got to
put him on a train. That make sense?"

"Damn right!"

"Chances are, Bria will be the one to take him
wherever they go. That gives me a shot at both of
'em."

"And the third one?"

"With luck, if they point him out to me."

They dozed facing the fire, listened to the noise
rising from the flats. Sid returned at nine, put Oscar
back on tether, filled his coffeecup, and squatted
down. Nellie said, "Johnson get in?"

"Just before dark, him, the rest of his outfit, about
a hundred more. All the ranchers are camped around
Johnson. Bunch of newspaper reporters came in, and
a whole load of folks from Omaha. The Brulé are on
the north bank, upstream from the mouth of Ribbon
Creek. Oglala are on the south bank opposite them.
Cheyenne River, Standing Rock, Lower Brulé, all on
the north bank below Ribbon Creek."

"The whole damn state is here!"

Sid grunted. "I feel something."

"In your bones?"

"My nose, Nellie."

"Then pay heed, by god! With your nose, you can't go wrong."

Sid grinned. "And a goodnight to you, you old rip!"

Badger heard music, an honest-to-god band playing music on the flats above the Cheyenne River on Thanksgiving eve in the year of somebody's lord, 1908. He said, "Whose band?" and Sid answered, "Brookings," and Nellie growled, "Shaddup!" and they slept in a night growing colder by the hour, woke when Lester called, "Breakfast!" to a thin gray sky, temperature so cold the snow hung overhead in the freezing air. It was a fine day for something: living, racing, dying. They ate quickly, saddled, harnessed the buckskins to Nellie's handy wagon, Badger sat with her while Sid and Lester escorted them down the slope through the bottoms onto the flats, part of a movement of hundreds converging on the race course. The Indians had come earlier and lined the course, sitting very close, from the starting line to the pile of rocks.

"Any bets yet, Sid?"

"Quite a few, Nellie."

They worked the handy wagon onto a little hump of earth between the starting line and the betting ground; standing, Badger could see the Sioux betting post at the north end of the ground, surrounded by little stacks of gold, silver and currency held in place with crossed rifles, revolvers, bridles, saddles, bankets, beadwork and a few lances. The first ponies were tied on the other side of the post. The county sheriff's deputies, the U.S. deputy marshals, and the Indian policemen were standing guard. Badger heard the Brookings band playing somewhere to the southeast, the sky was light gray and now snow was falling on a late morning still below freezing, as the crowd gath-

ered around the betting ground and the race course,
waiting for the people Pass Johnson had called "those
damned half-breeds," and for Johnson himself.

"Here they come!"

Up from the river came the mixed-bloods, a solid
block of riders pushing straight through the crowd to
the betting ground, spreading on both sides and lining
up six deep; then Badger saw the teams trotting side
by side, coming up the path from the river crossing,
riders on both flanks, two more teams and wagons
bringing up the rear, all four suddenly pulling off to
the west and forming a tight square with one small
entry facing the river. Twenty riders went through
the entry inside the square. Then another group of
riders came from the river, led by a big man riding a
black horse with a hackamore. Sid said:

"There's old Jules!"

Babine wore a high-crowned black Stetson, knee-
high winter moccasins, and a long sheepskin-lined
coat. He rode to the betting ground, legged off like a
boy, walked through the crowd to the restraining
rope, flanked and followed by twenty men. Sid
said, "Man on his right," and Badger saw a broad-
shouldered, deep-chested man in boots, overalls
and blanket coat, wide slash of mouth in a dark face,
hard brown eyes under the wide hat brim. "That's
Dan Bria. Jean Babine's on his left, five men left of
Jean is Little Joe Mulot."

"I recognize him, Sid."

Badger saw the young face, looked along the line,
saw the old man's blood in many faces. Whatever
they were doing inside that wagon square was hidden
from view; then voices called, "Here comes Johnson!"
and they saw the tall man lead at least two hundred
riders straight across the flats, through the crowd
around the starting line, to the south side of the betting ground. Pass Johnson was smoking a cigar, lean,
dark face shadowed under the fine gray Stetson, the
blue eyes shining, black moustache a solid color above
the soft blue shirt and black string tie, the dark suit,

high black boots, and the holster tucked inconspicu-
ously under the coat. Johnson dismounted, touched his
hat to Babine standing directly across the way,
looked around calmly for judges and starter. Pass
Johnson had a high, clear voice:

"Gentlemen, you ready?"

Two judges and the starter were standing on the
west side of the betting ground with the U.S. marshal
and the county sheriff. They nodded, the sheriff
swung on one heel and called:

"You all set, Jules?"

Babine spoke for the first time, "Talk or bet?"

Pass Johnson ducked under the rope. Babine
went under. They met in the middle of the betting
ground, flanked by their people, the judges, and the
starter. Pass Johnson said:

"Make your bet, Babine. I'll cover."

"Fine wit me."

Babine pulled two leather sacks from the left-hand
pocket of his coat and dropped them on the ground.
His people dropped sacks in front of Johnson's people.
Johnson said, "How much, Babine?"

"Ten, Mister."

Pass Johnson unbuttoned his coat, lifted a black
leather notecase from the inside pocket, counted
out ten one-thousand-dollar bills, laid them on the
ground beside the two leather sacks. Before he could
straighten, Babine dropped another sack.

"Five more, Mister?"

"Pleasure."

Johnson counted five more bills, placed them beside
the third sack, counted out five more, laid them on
the ground, and stood.

"Five more says you made a bad bet, Babine."

Babine reached into his right-hand pocket and
dropped a fourth sack.

"All bet, Mister."

All along the line, on both flanks, Babine's people
bet, Johnson's people called, bet, were called, bet
again, called a final time. Pass Johnson turned and

walked from the betting ground to the starting line, followed by Babine, judges and starter hurrying to take their positions, mount the horses held for them. The starter moved to his place on the left side of the scratched line in the dirt; one judge trotted down the course to examine the ground on his way to the turning rocks where the white sheet on the pole fluttered in the wind. He would take his position on the back southeast side of the rock pile, watch the racers make the turn, follow them around and see them double back for home. At the starting line, the remaining judge took his position on the right side of the line, facing the starter, and ordered the crowd to please give way at least six feet. When less than three was given, he blew a whistle, Indian police and sheriff's deputies came running; quietly, without force, they moved everyone back, giving starter, judges and racers plenty of room. The gray sky spat snow, the ground was still frozen, the wind was cold on a cold, gray day; the head judge nodded to Johnson, to Babine, and raised his left arm.

"Bring up the racers!"

Johnson's men split the crowd on the south side; coming through, protecting the blaze-faced sorrel from reaching hands, a dozen men led horse and rider forward. The sorrel's rider was a tall, slim man with long arms, powerful hands, and legs that gripped a horse's barrel with the strength of a wrestler applying a scissors; horse and man were a team, had ridden races for three years. The handlers brought them through, Johnson turned and smiled at his rider, the rider touched his hat and grinned behind the quirt held between his big yellow teeth. Johnson said, "That'll do, boys," and stopped them three lengths behind the starting line.

"Mr. Babine!" the judge called.

A gap opened in the wagon corral; through it came Dan Bria and Jean Babine, leading the mare, it too shielded on all sides by Babine men. Through the crowd to a position beside the sorrel, jockey sitting in the relaxed, slouched-back manner that only true jockeys achieved, that funny little sitting-squat on the lightweight saddle, short stirrups bringing his knees against the roach of the mane, back in a curved line from saddle seat to cap brim that nearly touched the hair between the mare's ears. Quirt in teeth, hands on reins, loose now, the mare held firmly by Bria and Jean Babine. Snapper wore a blue cap, blue flannel shirt, brown corduroy pants and moccasins. He sat the mare as if Mother Nature had sewn them together with seamless thread. He looked neither right nor left, up or down, stared at some spot just beyond the mare's flop ears, waiting for the business to get done and the walk-up to start.

The judge held a silver dollar in his cocked right thumb.

"Call it, gentlemen."

Johnson said, "Heads."

The dollar rose, spun, fell to earth.

"Tails."

"Your choice of position, Mr. Babine."

"Insite."

"Inside for the mare, outside for the sorrel. Gentlemen, are you ready?"

"Ready wit me."

"Gentlemen," Pass Johnson said quietly, "let me get somethin' straight. This is a race between my blaze-faced sorrel and Mr. Babine's mouse-colored, stocking-legged mare. Am I right, Babine?"

"*Oui!*"

"I'm ready to race my sorrel against Babine's mare any day in the week and twice on Sundays, but today being a holiday, and having bet a considerable sum of money, I want to be damn sure my horse is running against Babine's mare."

"What you mean, Mister?"

"Babine, I mean that ain't your mare!"

"Not my mare!" Babine roared.

"That's a ringer, Babine."

"No!"

"All right, if she ain't a ringer, you can't object to me and the judges lookin' her over."

Pass Johnson was suddenly facing Jean Babine and Bria, flanked by his picked men. The judge dismounted and pushed forward. Snapper sat the mare unmoving, hands tightening on the reins, knees gripping tighter. The judge said:

"That's a serious charge, Mr. Johnson."

"Judge, this mare is a ringer. Everybody here knows that Babine's mare has got two white front stockings. This mare has got two white front stockings. I got a white linen handkerchief here—" it appeared, snowy-white in his right hand, one of his people handed him a small can "—and this can in my other hand is filled with naphtha gas. I'm going to wet this handkerchief and rub those stockings off this mare."

Sid Hecht whispered, "Jesus H. Christ!"

"Grab your hats," Nellie grunted. "Stick close, Lester."

Pass Johnson knelt down, poured naphtha gas on the white handkerchief, took a firm grip on the right front foreleg, began rubbing downward with the hair —everyone within seeing range saw all or part of the same unbelievable transformation: the white stocking came off, underneath was a solid mouse-colored leg. The handkerchief was whiter than white with whatever coloring the ringer Rembrandt had used. Johnson turned to the judge and starter. "You want me to rub the left front off?" and the judge said, "This sure as hell is no white-stockinged mare. What's going on, Mr. Babine?"

Babine said, "Bah!" and suddenly the jockey on the mare came to life, had her spinning on her hind legs, faunching, coming down running straight through the crowd toward the wagon pen, a quick graceful jump over the tongue, through the gap inside; as the jockey in the blue cap vanished with the ringer mare, the gap opened a yard wider and out of the pen came a white-stockinged mare—

"By god!" Sid Hecht said, "the Babine mare!"

—stepping daintily on her white forelegs, picking her way through the crowd, guards fending off the curious, Bria and Jean Babine at her bits, guiding her; her rider sitting not as Snapper had sat the ringer, but straight up like an Indian, hat brim low over dark, thin face, chin strap tight under the round chin, wearing faded blue pants, patched yellow shirt, moccasins, hands holding reins and quirt, young by the sit. Nellie asked, "Who—?" and Sid Hecht said, "Got to be one of the grandkids, got to be," and the mare came up to the position inside, on the left of the blaze-faced sorrel, and Babine looked at mare, rider, turned to judge, starter and Pass Johnson:

"All right, Mister. You want to race, huh?"

"I'd shoot a man for lying," Pass Johnson said. "I can't blame a man for trying. Let's race."

Babine swung his hat above his head and shouted:

"Aller, Bebel Aller!"

The sorrel and the mare began the walk-up, breath throwing foam flecks, eyes rolling, starter's eye on them, trigger finger tightening as they approached the line, three steps, all even, two steps, his knuckle whitened, one step, on the line, the shot sounded, the mare was half a jump ahead of the sorrel, the clouds above rolled back and the sun shone through, off and running between the lines of people, over the frozen prairie, the thin white snowfall, in the roar of the crowd rising as the clods ripped behind the sharp-caulked shoes. The white flag on the rock-pile pole beckoned, the youngster on the mare was flattened along the neck now, the mare was flying, the sorrel came through that snowdust, one length behind, then a gain to the mare's tail, around the rock pile in two tight turns, both holding, sorrel at the mare's flank, now the stirrup, reaching for the neck, crowd up, Indians standing, the blaze-faced sorrel was head and head with Babine's mare, the tall man in the saddle used his quirt for the first time, gave the sorrel

a warning crack, and the sorrel came out of its gather
with that famous explosion of speed; but the youngster on the mare was shouting, hat back, mouth wide,
words slashed away by wind, as the mare stretched,
her stride lengthened, she drew away from the sorrel's head, cleared the neck, now she was truly flying, so low and so fast she had that ghostly shadow
look of the deer in the trees, she ran away from the
sorrel in the sorrel's moment of greatest speed,
crossed the line a length ahead and still gaining, was
past everyone down the open stretch across the flats
toward the bottoms, turning under the rein, curving,
slowly easing off, still running, moving straight on
down toward the river crossing where fifty mixed-
blood riders waited, all hit the water, were obscured
as they crossed, climbed the north bank, vanished into the trees; while all eyes were on the sorrel and the
mare, Babine had disappeared, the rest of his people had moved backward across the betting ground,
picking up the winnings as their wave receded, the
wagon pen dissolved, the teams galloped, the Indians
rose up and flooded the betting ground, collecting
their bets, moved in a solid mass toward the river behind Babine's people before anyone could object, if
objection was possible, for after all, as judges and
starter agreed, it was a race fairly run and fairly won,
and that was the end of it, unspoken was the fact
that nobody could follow Babine and his people,
and the Indians across the river onto reservation
ground without a permit. The snowdust was still in
the air, time was suspended, within those moments
of regaining breath and composure, people started
talking, the arguments began, the legend was born
and weaned on the race course ground in the last
notes of falling snow: how did Babine do it? How did
he beat the Johnson sorrel with that little mare?

Badger took the reins and drove Nellie's team after Sid and Lester, Nellie holding on tightly, looking
back toward the river and the crowd that wandered

over the flats in a kind of daze, unable to accept the
blistering finish to such a long trip, the human drama
gone, the race run and won, in less time than it took
to describe. Nellie got down, sat on a box facing the
fire, and blurted, "Too sudden, nobody's geared to get
chopped off so fast." Then roused herself, made sandwiches and coffee, they sat eating and drinking,
watching the scene below, what time was it? Only one-
thirty, most of an afternoon left, what to do?

Badger said, "You all get started."

"You want help?"

"No thanks, Sid. My battle now."

"Lester and me better get under way," Nellie
said. "Birdie's holding down the fort alone."

Lester said, "What will they do, Henry?"

"No idea, Lester. Got to watch, let them move."

He stood beside the fire and waved Sid off, helped
Lester load the handy wagon, gave Nellie an arm
up, waved goodby as she swung round and followed
Lester up the ridge. He was back where he started;
and across the river were Snapper, Bria and that
third, unknown man. Cat at the mousehole; all he had
to do was wait.

Working leisurely, he repacked his wagon, harnessed the paints, drove carefully along the ridge to
the middle fork, followed it to its springheads, went
on to the top of the ridge and stopped in a wind
blowout beyond the edge where he could sit on a
rock and look down at the river. Weather was building up in the north, scattered snow fell across the
valley, gave strength to the race-goers who packed
and began moving out of the flats, the bottoms, up
the river and down the river; by sunset the flats were
empty, everyone was on the road. Badger ate sandwiches, drank water, wrapped himself in a blanket
and resumed his vigil. The paints, fed and blanketed,
stood behind the wagon out of the wind that blew
cold as the night was turning. Today might be the
last day of the year to race horses and feel the heat-

less sun. They would not make a move from Babine's,
but he did expect them at dawn.

He watched the small cavalcade of wagons, riders,
and led horses come from the river crossing and line
out on the Pierre road. Two big teams pulling two
wagons, ten riders, eight led horses: all came on,
grew in his lenses, until he saw two men on the lead
wagon seat, slid back, refocused, saw two men on the
second wagon seat. One big man dressed in bulky
winter clothes; beside him another man equally tall,
not so heavyset, wearing heavy clothes and eyeglasses
with colored lenses. They were heading south, making
a beeline for the railroad, would likely rest after midnight and go straight through tomorrow. If he drove
a parallel route, he could match their pace, keep
them in sight; beyond that he dared not think or
plan. Watching, he saw them halt to check gear before the long climb; the man with the colored lenses
got down and walked back toward the led horses.
Still no sign of Snapper.

Snapper spoke through the flaps after Whitey got
down.

"Who's up there in the peanut gallery, Trader?"

"Can't make him out. Can guess."

"What was it the Indians called him?"

"Iruka."

"Yeh—is it him?"

"No matter, he can't come in here."

"Can we go out there?"

"Got no reason. We'll take it easy tonight, tomorrow
we hit the railroad, load Whitey and the mare on the
first train east *or* west, you if you want to go—"

"Trader, I think I wore out my welcome."

"Not with us."

"He don't think so."

"Badger don't know nothin'. He's just guessing. You
take it easy, I'll see you safe on your way."

Snapper grinned and lay down in his blanket bed.

Last night was one to remember, the first time in his life that everything he planned, and helped do, turned out even better than he dared hope for. The kid had run and won a race as good as any rider in the world could have run the flop-eared mare. Whitey had done a ringer job that nobody had tried before, pulled it off without a hitch, in front of a mean and sharp-eyed bunch of men who really knew horses. And himself? He had brought the Indian mare out, handled her exactly right, moved at the precise moment, then had the absolutely wonderful feeling of watching the kid make it all come true. Talk about a night! The weight in the money belt around his waist had increased plenty since yesterday. Old Babine had said, "Snap, you earn every cent!" and filled his hands with double eagles until they spilled over and rolled on the floor. But the best part was watching the ugly duckling in that bunch of mother hens with all their pretty spring fryers. He was in his cabin, washing up for supper, when somebody knocked. He called, "It ain't locked!" and she slipped inside, closed the door, and stood there looking at him. Snapper said, "By god, kid!" and saw her wearing a dress for the first time. Instead of trying to be polite, or drum up a lot of fancy words, Snapper forgot all that and spoke his thoughts:

"Kid, you look great!"

"You mean it, Snapper?"

"I don't butter no burnt toast, kid."

"Snapper, will you dance with me tonight?"

Snapper said, "I ain't tripped the light fantastic for so long, I don't remember which foot goes first, but I'll try if you teach."

"I can't dance, Snapper."

"Who says?"

"I ain't never tried."

"Well, by god! We'll ride that horse together!"

Then she was overcome with the dress, the shoes, and her combed hair tied with ribbons. She turned and ran out the door across the yard toward the house. Snapper closed the door, sat on the cot, and rubbed his smiling face with his rough, scarred hands and tried to remember how a man acted at a dance with a young lady in a lovely dress. No use—he'd never attended one when he was young. Oh, he'd danced plenty in the glory years, and all the girls said he was a fine stepper, but that was when he usually was too drunk to remember. Well, tonight he'd be sober as a judge and twice as nice as anybody else. The kid had it coming.

Snapper stole a half-hour snooze, dressed, and went back to the house, so jam-packed with family, relatives, friends, and Indians that it took an hour to go from front to rear. Half the tribes were camped around, their fires were lighting up the sky. When Snapper came in, about ten of the Babine's grandchildren hoisted him up and carried him to the big table and gave him a dozen cheers that hurt his ears. He took a small drink from the offered bottle, grinned, and shook hands with everybody who came to pat his back and make him feel at home. When the meal started, Babine took the head of the table, and the kid was on his left hand in the woman's place of honor, where no woman had sat since Babine's wife died. Whitey was on his right, Jean Babine and Bria next to him, and they put Snapper beside the kid. It was a big moment for the kid. Snapper knew enough about the way things ran to appreciate Babine's gesture. When dinner was finished, everybody helped clear the room for dancing. The players tuned up, Xavier tapped his right foot twice, and the music welled. Babine danced with Rose, everybody clapped, then her father, then she turned and took Snapper's hand, led him out, and Snapper took a timid sliding step, discovered he could still trip a couple of simple movements; all at once it came back and he danced her around the floor very gently, knowing what was happening to her. She was becoming a woman. Maybe it wouldn't last long enough to

get her out of here, meet some nice young man—
Snapper laughed, she looked up and said, "What for,
Snapper?" and Snapper said, "Because I feel good,
kid. For me, for you, for all of us."

All day Friday the sun broke through the clouds on little visits that made up in looks what they lacked in warmth. Late that afternoon from a high ridge to the west, Badger saw the Babine outfit leave the Pierre road and turn south on the trail that passed Flapjack Nellie's en route to Wendte, the railroad town on Bad River. Badger drove the paints hard, pulled into Nellie's barn minutes before sunset, hotfooted across the backyard to the kitchen where Nellie waited, holding the door.

"On my heels, Nellie."

"Want to trip 'em up here?"

"Show me a pole."

"How about the three up front right now, U.S. marshal and two deputies."

"What's his name?"

"Don't know, Henry."

"I'll take a peek first."

"Try this for size—" Nellie handed him a newspaper, her finger on the story "—Mike sent it up, got here yesterday."

The Omaha *World-Herald* story, reprinted from the Ophelia *Plainsman*, related the strange and violent death of one Pat O'Doul. There was no doubt about the manner of the ex-pugilist's demise, but spectators were quoted as saying that O'Doul had evidently been scared half out of his wits by some-

138

thing or someone unknown in the waning minutes of the championship water fight. The balance of the story told how O'Doul was killed.

"Nellie, if the Babines stop, can you get Snapper and Bria to read this?"

"Just give me the high-sign."

Badger ran to the barn, asked a favor of Lester, ran along the west side of the house to the front corner, in time to watch the Babine outfit pull in. He saw Jean Babine, Bria, the tall man with the colored eyeglasses, and Snapper follow the other men inside. He gave them a minute to get settled before walking over to look closely at teams, saddle horses, and the led string. Almost hidden by the larger horses, a smaller one stood quietly in a full wool suit, fine buttoned blanket and long hood edged in black braid. Badger saw two flop ears hanging from the hood holes, felt the bridle beneath, rubbed buttonholes bound with chamois skin, saddle cinched under the blanket. Snugged down but ready, the ringer was going home. Lester spoke from the darkness:

"Bay's tied on the east side."

"Thanks, Lester."

"Birdie's on the roof."

"What for?"

"Help, if you need it."

"With what?"

"The ten-gauge."

"Dammit—l"

But Lester had gone. Badger circled, took the narrow westside hallway to the anteroom that opened into the big dining and bar room, looked through the beaded curtain and saw three men at the near corner table. Nellie had no idea how badly a U.S. marshal named Howard wanted to trip up a whiskey-runner named Badger, not because Badger sold whiskey to the Sioux, but because a half-breed sold whiskey to the Sioux and was too smart for U.S. marshals and government agents. On the other hand, why not use Howard as a trip pole? The rest of Badger's eggs

were in one round oak basket: Jean Babine, the tall
man, Bria, and Snapper sat at the table between bar
and front door, other Babines filled the far end of
the room. When Nellie sailed by with the beer pitcher, Badger murmured, "In here!" and on her return
trip she stepped through the beads. Badger spoke into
her ear:

"That's Howard, marshal from Winner, hates my
guts."

"Damn!"

"Let's use him, Nellie."

"How?"

"Go back, get them reading the newspaper story."

"Done."

"I'll come out to the end of the bar and catch
Howard's eye. From then on, it's my fight."

Snapper ate roast beef, mashed potatoes, hot biscuits, and stewed tomatoes. The red-headed woman
refilled their beer glasses and grinned at Jean.

"Helluva race, huh?"

"You see it?"

"Damn tootin'! That sorrel sure ate your dust."

"You bet?"

"Never got the chance. Your Pa was making John-
son jig too fast. Reminds me of another contest—"
Nellie scooped a newspaper off the bar, laid it beside
Jean's plate "—read this one, damnedest thing I ever
heard of, happened at that big water fight out in
Ophelia—"

"Nellie!"

"Hold your water, boys, I'm comin'!"

Snapper watched her march to the far corner table, refill glasses, speak to the sandy-haired man with
the pale blue eyes; as she hurried away Jean Babine
said, "Some way to die," and passed the newspaper
to Bria who read the story and pushed it under
Snapper's left hand.

"Not tonight, Trader. I'm cross-eyed."

"Better read it, best eye-hook you'll find."

Something in Bria's voice made Snapper raise the newspaper and read; and then his appetite turned to dust. Bria murmured, "End of the bar," and Snapper looked over the paper, recognized Badger, pushed his chair back a cautious inch, felt along his left leg for the knife in his boot.

"Let's take him, Trader!"

"See the man going over beside him?"

"Sure, hell with him."

"That's Howard, U.S. marshal, two deputies at their table. Sit tight."

Bria wiped his mouth, rose, strolled to the last table where Rose sat hidden among the young men. He leaned down and spoke in her ear, "Trouble, watch me," and returned to his table. Two chairs stood empty, Snapper had gone. Badger had vanished from the end of the bar.

"Jean, where's Snapper?"

"Guess he had to go."

Jean was Dan Bria's blood brother, by marriage and by secret ceremony, but Bria dared not tell Jean the truth and ask for help. He said, "Me too," and stepped outside, let his eyes adjust, saw Snapper pretending to tighten the tarp ropes on the camp wagon. Bria rotated his left shoulder to loosen the knife sheath, stepped forward, heard a young voice speak directly overhead, "You stop there, Mister!" Bria stopped. Snapper moved from the camp wagon into the mass of saddle horses, started doing something Bria could not see until one animal backed into view, wool suit peeling forward over saddle, shoulders, neck and head, following the hood into Snapper's hands. Snapper mounted so smoothly that Bria blinked once and there he was, cheek on neck, mare steady as rock under his familiar touch. Movement swam into the far left corners of Bria's eyes, Badger came toward the wagons at the exact moment Snapper guided the mare through the saddle horses toward the road; all were indistinct ghosts for three heartbeats. Then the mare ran and Badger passed

Bria as if he did not exist, whipped around the east corner of the house, reappeared seconds later on a big bay that crossed the yard and angled onto the east road. Bria heard a faint, fading rataplan of hoof-beats, realized that Snapper had not taken the Wendte trail south, but stayed on the Fort Pierre–Black Hills road. Was Snapper trying to toll Badger away, give the others a chance to clear before he lost Badger on the fastest mare that ever ran these grasslands? Bria spoke calmly:

"All right to move?"

The voice cracked through a range from low soprano to high tenor, "Go back inside, Mister."

Bria returned to his table, studied the room, forced his voice low, "Snapper just cut and run for the river."

Jean Babine said, "What the hell for?"

"No idea. He took the mare."

Whitey Crosier was out the front door, across the yard in a blur, picking a saddle horse, gone down the road before Jean Babine and Bria reached the wagons. Jean cursed softly.

"Them goddamn marshals!"

"What they do?"

"When you went back to Rose's table, that marshal went over to Badger, and he look straight at us, say something, and that marshal curl his lips and look at us and say something nasty. Next thing—whoosh!—Snapper he go out the door. Let's go!"

"Where?"

"God damn! Good question, that. Let's follow Whitey and see, eh?"

If Snapper was thinking logically, he would slow his pace on the strange road, let the mare get the feel of the ground and set her own pace. Badger could not match her speed, but the bay horse was fresh while the mare was still recovering from her winning run on the flats. Worst of all, for Snapper, if he reached Fort Pierre and missed his road leading to the river crossing, he would inevitably follow the route all strangers took and ride straight into a box. The mare was not a working horse; she was a lovely piece of machinery, delicate and intricate. She could be ruined by one stone, one stick, one bog-down. Surely, if Snapper took time to think, he would double back.

But the mare ran on. The bay had strength and pride, felt solid under Badger's legs as he responded willingly and lost very little ground. Badger wondered if he should make a try at stopping Snapper; at the midway bend, the straight entering town, in town itself? If Snapper missed the approach road to the river crossing, he would likely cross the railroad tracks, run through town and find himself on the old bottom road that squeezed through the thickets to the abandoned steamboat landing dock. Riding, Badger thought of the trick that sent Snapper rushing into this predicament. Just by coming to the bar and speaking, showing how he felt about half-breeds, Howard had reacted as Badger hoped: glared at Jean Babine's table when Badger identified them as the race-ringer outfit. Snapper broke, jumped up, walked out the front door. Badger walked away through the beaded curtain, ran down the side hall, around the house into the front yard. If Howard ever learned how he had been used, he'd come after Badger with a club. In his own way, the marshal was as stupid as the jockey who had watched him and assumed that his words were meant for no one else.

Badger could not tell if it was the road, an owl, the bay horse, or the other factor that killed men and horses along the river in the winter when the air holes bred just beneath the ice. If a hot-blooded horse was suddenly thrown off balance, got scared, mad, or both, and started fanning the breeze, that horse could—and often had—run himself to death. If a hot-blooded horse became crazed toward the end of a long run, so tired he was unaware of danger, he could easily run out on river ice, go through an air hole, and never be seen again. Uncle Bad Knees had always claimed that the worst medicine for a hot-blooded horse was a rider who lost his head and let his fear enter the horse. The bay had crept nearer, proof that Snapper was not listening for pursuit, had eased off to catch his own breath, or was so frightened he had lost his sense of pace and filled the mare with his fear. Whatever triggered the explosion—a clod spinning off the bay's shoes, an owl, road sound, it caused the mare to leap with a scream so that only a rider of Snapper's great skill could stick her saddle. Snapper tried to calm her, but her hot blood betrayed her, she got the bit in her teeth and began running down the road toward Fort Pierre, out of terrible fear into madness, out of madness into total insanity. The bay ran hard, lost a little ground, gained some back when the flying mare slipped and nearly tumbled.

Badger saw the lights, tried to call warning, came off the high ground past the river-crossing turn over the railroad tracks through the middle of town into the trees where the wagon road narrowed as it wound toward the willow thickets. The mare struck a puddle, splashed muddy water, cracked thin ice, bang-banged over an ancient stretch of corduroy, plowed through soft sand to the foot of the dock, sounded like a runaway rolling up loose bridge planks on some final crossing; out the long dock to the end where she made a soaring leap and hit the water. The channel was swollen with the late fall rise, lumpy with deadheads, snags, stumps, all rolling downstream in the surging Missouri current that whirled the mare like a toy and sent Snapper flying beyond reach of rein or stirrup, into the icy water of early winter, warmly dressed, money belt crammed with double eagles hugged tight around his waist. The current gave Snapper a sucking yank that made him feel the dead weight of his luck around his waist; he clawed at his belt, his buttons, to lighten the golden load, but an old cottonwood butt on a long journey to nowhere tickled his feet in its frieze of sodden roots, pulled him down and under and around, twenty feet deep in a forty-foot channel, dropped him, let him roll on with the rip, like countless horses and many men, he might bob up next spring and he might not. But he was a lucky man. How many went to their maker with the wherewithal to live the richest possible life in whichever world was reserved for horse's best friend.

And the mare? Rider gone, her fear died with the cold water that scythed her legs, flipped her, gave her legs back as she rolled downstream, tail spread out behind in a wet fan that acted as a makeshift rudder, helped her lift her head and blow her nostrils clear, expel all the muddy water, pull clean air into her lungs, start her walking-swimming, looking and feeling for the nearest ground. She had enough strength to push her right shoulder against the side-swiping current, swim in that direction until she heard a voice. She doubled her effort, struck mud that dissolved underfoot, made six more fierce, plunging steps that brought her onto sand, then stones, she heard the voice again as she limp-legged onto the upper tip of a sandbar that thrust out from the west bank. Standing in the cold night, she shivered and groaned, smelled another horse, saw the bay and the man coming toward her. The man talked nonsense while he took off his coat and draped it over the mare's neck and shoulders, wrenched her saddle into position so the cinches stopped binding her. Then bay horse and man led the mare along the sandbar to the river bank, through the willow thickets and the bottoms, along the old road to town, straight to the livery barn where the night man sprang into action.

Whitey Crosier galloped into town minutes after the mare was dried, rubbed down, blanketed, and fed a hot toddy. He went over her with eyes and fingers, sniffed the hot toddy and made her finish the basin, thanked the night man for excellent work. The night man told how he saw the mare and rider run through town and take the old steamboat dock road, fol-

lowed by the man who brought her in. Who was he?
No idea who, he rode a bay horse and he sure as hell
pulled her from the river because jesus! you could
hear her scream a mile when she went off the
end of the dock. Where was this man? Why, soon as
he saw the mare was all right, he left. Where was the
mare's rider? The night man shook his head and
pointed to the river.

Badger met a wagon and several riders on the
way to Nellie's. Nellie and Birdie came running to
meet him, but Badger beat them to the first question:
"Where's Lester?"
"Chasing Bria—what happened?"
Badger told them.
"No chance for Snapper?"
"None."
"Now what?"
"Follow Lester."
"All hell broke loose after you took out."
"What happened, Nellie?"
"Howard tried to arrest somebody for something
but couldn't invent any charge that fit anybody. Jean
Babine got his bunch headed after that tall feller with
the colored glasses, and Lester played a hunch. He
scooted across the pasture to the turnoff and, sure
enough, he saw Bria's wagon, Bria driving, one other
rider and four led horses, all take the Wendte road
while the rest of the bunch headed east for Fort
Pierre, Howard and them deputies of his hot on their
trail. Lester saddled the pinto and set sail after Bria."
"Can you fix me some lunch, Nellie?"
"How much time?"
"While Birdie and me hitch up."
"Go to it!"
Badger and Birdie harnessed the paints, hitched
up, checked the gear; twenty minutes later Badger
was eating his supper on the Wendte road. Just before sunrise he met Lester coming north with the
news: Bria had bought boxcar space to Rapid City

and piled his outfit onto a westbound freight two hours ago.

"You read the train board, Lester?"

"Sure did, next westbound freight's at eight—hey! wait a minute, Henry!"

Badger turned on the seat, cupped one ear.

"What happened to Snapper?"

"Pretty sure he drowned."

"You don't know for sure?"

"Lester, I'm no catfish."

10

The westbound freight, Number 19, stopped in all the lonely little towns. Wendte, Van Metre, Midland, Nowlin; in each Badger leaned out his boxcar doorway and saw the brakeman's no-spot signal. Powell, Philip and Cottonwood fell behind the Baldwin 4–6–0, wind curled the greasy black smoke along the cars; an hour into darkness the train slowed, squealed to full halt in Quinn. Badger saw the lantern bob, heard the brakeman call:

"Seventeen dropped your outfit in the hole."

Nineteen spotted Badger's boxcar on the siding, the brakeman eased the grain door gangway over the gap between unloading dock and boxcar doorway, helped Badger hitch up and prybar the wagon around the corner across the gangway onto the dock. Badger drove down the ramp, stuck a bill in the brakeman's pocket, and over-rode his protest.

"Drinks on me, your whole crew."

"All right, thanks."

"My thanks to you."

Nineteen hooked up and snored away; yellow windowlight beckoned. Badger drove across the tracks to the store, bought supplies, asked about the other wagon outfit. Sure, headed south that afternoon. Badger got permission to sleep in the barn; at four a.m. wind shredded his departure sounds, nobody saw him go in full darkness. He drove south on the Big Foot trail,

got down at daybreak, walked beside the familiar
wheel marks, recognized the bay team's shoes,
counted one saddle and four led horses. Would Bria
stay on the Big Foot trail through the badlands, cross
White River near the mouth of Yellow Medicine
Creek, and run straight for Pine River Agency? If
he did, Badger was in trouble, left so far behind the
dust would settle before he could taste it. The tracks
suddenly turned east into the heart of the badlands.
Proof of what? That Bria was not welcome at Pine
Ridge?

Hours later the paints cakewalked around a seephole; the Oglala bow lance was shoved into the damp
alkali mud between the wagon tracks. Badger yanked
it up, ran a thumb along the warped quills, felt the
loop notches and the spearhead seat; not much
of a lance but it told him what Bria and the other
rider wanted him to believe: if he came on, it was
to the death. Badger didn't believe a word of it. Bria
didn't want to fight anybody to the death. He wanted
to spend that ringer race money, not have it tomb-
stoned above his grave. Badger broke the old lance
over his clenched thigh and tossed the pieces into
the seephole. Time to camp, make an early start. He
had not seen the badlands since the fall of 1903
when he helped Sid Hecht chase a bunch of stolen
horses. His uncle swore that the best way to remember bad country was close your eyes and paint
that country inside your head. Badger closed his eyes
and told memory to pick the colors, start painting
the inside of his skull as bold-bright as a new Bull
Durham ad on the side of a red barn.

Memory began where the south fork of White
River came into the main channel about seventy miles
east and a bit south of where he slept; drew a line
north to mark the eastern boundary. From that line,
for some ninety miles west, the north bank of White
River was shut in by the high wall of the Big Badlands.
North of those crenellated buttes the country became
a crumple of hills, ridges, ravines, valleys, and white

alkali flats strewn with the bones of prehistoric monsters nobody had ever seen alive. South boundary of the badlands, White River ran through white clay beds in its upper valley, and certain seasons of the year saw the water milky white, but the river most likely got its name from the clouds of white dust that swept along the valley in dry, windy weather. When the Sioux entered the country, the badlands were full of animals and birds; from them came the elk-horns and buffalo horns found around the blackened fire hubs of forgotten hunters. Then the white man came, camps were littered with rusty tin cans and brass shell cases and broken whiskey bottles. Cattle and horses ran wild, impossible to catch where half the creeks were cut so deeply that horse and man could not cross, where some hills were so rough that a horse could not get over them. Men got lost in the badlands, died of heat, cold, thirst, and starvation. The Oglala called the badlands the home of the spirits, a land too bad even for them.

Bria sniffed the night and signaled halt. They made camp in a draw that flared the wind and hid their fire. Rose did her chores, started supper, sat hugging her legs, wishing she could find out what happened to Snapper. If he kept his promise, he had gone south with Whitey to lay up until spring.

"Father, you think he got away?"

"On that mare? Easy!"

"Maybe Badger won't find us."

"We got to be sure."

"Go east, split up?"

"Like I told you. I take the horses, you take the wagon."

"You sure he'll trail you, Father?"

"You bet."

"Where you goin' first?"

Bria drew a finger map in the dirt. "Since we come here last, that Milwaukee Railroad built west along White River. I'll cross it, go to the slick rocks, follow

the north bank upstream. You go north from here,
double back to the dugout—you sure you can unload?"

"Yes, Father."

"Wipe out the tracks, meet me north of Sheep
Mountain in five days."

"Father, if he comes, we kill him?"

"First we make him think we don' know he comes.
Then we set the trap."

"Who shoots?"

"You want to, Rose?"

She nodded, but she knew then that he was uncertain.

He found Bria's camp, tracked them east through
ravines and time-ravaged hills into a place where all
the rock once far beneath the surface had been
pushed upward and out until it fell over in rough
slabs; wind and water had niched, ditched, and crev-
iced the slabs, filled those pocks with grains of dirt
from which tiny pines now grew. In the middle of
the jumble, the Bria team and wagon went north,
the five horses turned south. The saddle-horse tracks
had deeper indents going south. Bria was the heavier man; was it invitation, challenge, trap? Bria
wanted him to follow, lose time, there was no way to
get his wagon down the wall to the river. But Bria
had forgotten one change.

Badger followed the horse tracks until they went
under a ravine trestle on the new Milwaukee Railroad
that ran west from Chamberlin along Medicine Creek
and through the badlands to Rapid City. Badger drove
east on the raw, year-old contractor's supply path
paralleling the right-of-way to the first town, made a
deal with the agent, backed his wagon into the barn
behind the station, saddled one paint, packed the
other, headed west on his own back-trail; reached the
trestle at four o'clock and followed Bria's tracks
until night caught him nowhere. Good as anywhere
else to close-hobble and cold-camp. He walked at
dawn, leading the paints, working out his aches and

pains through country starting to rear up and stand on end. Bria led his horses through narrow slots in bulging walls, over shale rock, up slick clay slopes onto a flat-topped butte that looked down on White River and south toward the Pine Ridge. Bria's trail vanished on the rock but iron horseshoes left a knick trail down the west flank of the butte into a shallow canyon soon squeezed into a chute floored with stones cobbled smooth by water. The chute became a tunnel that bored through solid rock toward the dirty gray light of a dim keyhole. Badger took short halter grips, led the paints until the keyhole grew horse-sized, popped paints and man onto a gravel beach above the water; ripples made a long arc across White River to the south bank, the beach stretched thirty feet along the river, necked into a narrow path invisible from above. More shoe knicks on rock showed Bria's line of flight upstream, but it was foolish to dare an unknown path in darkness.

Badger slept undisturbed through a freezing cold night into a colder, windy morning; across the river a north wind churned the shallows into scallops, blew snow flurries through bare trees, lost the battle to forming ice. Badger led the paints all day on that narrow path, stopped at sunset facing a heavy rock shoulder that hid all view upstream, and cold-camped in a cave. At dawn he scouted around the corner and saw the mouth of Yellow Medicine Creek across the river. Bria's tracks swung northwest in the general direction of the high, dry plateau country at the base of Sheep Mountain. Now, if he, Badger, was off to the north driving a camp wagon, with orders to meet Bria somewhere west of the Big Foot trail in a given number of days, where would he proceed to keep that rendezvous? Badger tipped his hat so-long to Bria and veered off north, struck a creek and ascended it to the Milwaukee tracks where, according to his new map, the equally new tank stop of Imlay was about five miles west. He rode the tracks into sight of town lights, circled, took another creek upstream, climbed a high butte, and stole a few hours' sleep before dawn.

Rose drove north and west from the upended rocks, threaded the big camp wagon through the badlands, over rocks, through water, rubbed out tire marks and team tracks with small unraveled gunnysack mops, crossed and recrossed the big creek six times approaching the cottonwood grove in the wishbone curve where the creek ran between twenty-foot straight-sided cutbanks; unloaded the camp wagon and lugged every sack, pack and bale up the rough log-ladder stairway into the dugout. It took most of the day to stack, repair the door hinges, clean the chimney flue in the rock pipe, and cook a hot meal. After supper she opened her pack, laid out the dress she wore at the party, looked at it while she cleaned her rifle beside the dying fire. She slept three hours, closed up, and drove to meet her father. On the morning of the fifth day she crossed the Big Foot trail and slipped into an unknown path that meandered southwest toward Sheep Mountain. Rifle beside her, knife in the sheath strapped to her left forearm, pretty dress forgotten; she urged the bays onward, face grim-set against the bitter wind.

Badger fixed an observation post on the northeast corner of the high butte. He drove four sticks into the ground, hung his gray blanket loosely, sprinkled dirt and pine needles on top, crawled underneath and wiggled into a comfortable position. Focusing his binoculars, he began searching the country from north to east in regular sweeps; by noontime he had seen everything but a camp wagon. Rabbits hopped nearby, sage hens scratched in a dust pocket, cattle and horses wandered in all sectors of his search lune. Shortly past noon he saw the camp wagon in a gap between two low hills, driver urging the bay team, wagon clipping along merrily where no road appeared to the naked eye. The binoculars picked up lines and occasional bank shadows of an old path as Badger watched the wagon pass east of his butte and vanish around the next hill on a southwest course. He folded his blanket, moved to the opposite corner of the butte top, and waited; the dirty-white canvas top appeared, wound on through the hills toward the distant blur of the plateau country at the base of Sheep Mountain. Badger watched it out of sight, stared at the rough-barked pines, and wondered where Bria was, *this moment*, waiting for that wagon.

There were a thousand hiding places along the north rim of the plateau. Trees, deadfalls, caves, rocks; the man who knew his ground could go to it and lie doggo for weeks on end, watching the country below. Bria saw the camp wagon approach in the style he had taught his daughter, a run south, a drift west, a little flutter east, always using the best ground, always edging nearer the real target while seeming to go elsewhere. When Rose stopped in the valley three miles north of his position on the rim and set up camp, Bria walked across the plateau corner to the horses staked in the trees on a western slope. He laced a pair of moccasins over his felt boots, wrapped his rifle breech in deerskin, and started north off the plateau as the sun went down. An hour later, in the trees on the south slope of the little valley, Bria tapped two stones together, counted three, tapped twice more. Rose gave her coffeepot a shake. Ten minutes later she climbed into the camp wagon and doused her lantern; two hours passed before she slipped through the trees and squatted beside him.

"See him, Father?"

"No sign—you?"

"Nothing. You think he come?"

"Know soon—go to the spring like we planned."

During the night Badger rode from the high butte across the Milwaukee tracks, on down to the west talus slopes of Sheep Mountain. He led the paints up the long ridges onto the middle ledges; from there it was mean climbing, man and horses scrambling over loose rock, making short jumps across little gaps and low spots, coming at last to the highest ledge on the northwest flank of the peak. Badger close-hobbled the paints in the trees, took a position between two massive boulders, and focused on the world below. Gray morning sky, mist across the plateau, bitter wind cutting his face. The first moving object he saw was a band of wild horses on the middle ledges below him. They looked so fine, and died so sadly when caught. Sid Hecht claimed that the best-looking stud a man ever saw on a hill turned into crowbait if you tried to rope and break him. Wild horses ran themselves to death rather than submit to rope and saddle, but there were always a few fools who packed into the badlands every year and spent a month proving what Sid told them before they invested their time and money. Sid called them lemonheads because they reminded him of the soldiers around the posts who used to drink lemon extract when they ran out of whiskey.

The black stud tensed, looked north, ran west with his mares; up from the lower tableland onto the plateau came the camp wagon, driver leaning forward, hat pulled low, feet braced, urging the bay team through loose sand, over shale rock, across the rough plateau to the spring in the trees at the eastern rimpoint. Badger wasted little time watching the driver who spent his daylight hours in the trees. Badger watched the country north and northwest as far as eye could see and lens extend vision; on the third morning the driver hitched up his bay team and drove off the plateau toward the Big Foot trail. Badger started to rise but something held him still as time on a dying man's breath. He dozed away the morning, ate cold lunch, watched the day turn mealy-gray; after dark he unpacked the remainder of his supplies: half a bushel of oats, enough food to last two weeks if

he took another notch in his belt. He had a hunch
that told him to stay where he was for one week, start
no fires after dark, make no careless moves day *or*
night. If Bria did not appear, it was his turn to move.
Nothing else fit the shape of things. Uncle Bad Knees
would call him crazy, but nod agreement.

Bria caught fleeting glimpses of the white wagon
top as Rose drove east. He walked around the big
hill and moved his horses lower down the north
flank into thicker timber. He sat beside his pack,
cleaned his rifle, changed socks, and returned to his
watch. Sitting against a tree, totally hidden in shadows, Bria had time to think and remember. In his
young days he had been an expert at losing battles;
if there was a way, he furnished wish, will, and his
own private brand of rushing in where fools fell back.
He was becoming what his cousin Philipe called him
one night while they were drinking in a dive on
the Fort Yates road. Philipe called him a stupid,
dirty, half-assed half-breed who didn't have the sense
to pour piss from a boot. Hell, Philipe added gen-
erously, Dan Bria oughta been a *wintke*, then maybe
he'd have a few friends. Bria hit his cousin on the
nose and they had such a good fight it sobered him
up. He thanked Philipe for doing what he had never
been able to do himself: think straight. Three years
later he married Isabelle, Rose was born the next
year, by then he had learned four things about himself: he was still, would always be, a half-breed.
When he took the time to use it, he had a good mind.
He was not dirty. And he had always been good
with horses. Old Jules Babine never did entirely trust
him, but Jean became his blood brother and consid-
ered him as much a family man as anybody else.

He started trading horses, made his first timid
venture east of the river and discovered that people
on farms, in small towns and little cities were easier
to trade with than his own kind. He made a good
living on the county-fair and race-meet circuits, but

it wasn't until Rose grew big enough to come with him that he found his real talent. He could pick a sucker, roll him clean, and be long gone before the sucker woke up with a headache. Rose had a natural feel for the business; together they learned the wisdom of ignoring little fish, waiting for the fat bullheads. Bria had waited patiently to get inside the Badger house, but that summer's big job was helping find a jockey for Whitey's ringer mare. Then Punch and Snapper came along, Bria passed the word and sized them up while Jean and Whitey got a line on Snapper's past. The old chief died, Jean made a special trip to Yankton on the last day of the meet to say that Whitey wanted Snapper, but Bria must have a tight rein on him to make sure he obeyed orders. Bria promised to deliver the goods, everything worked out better than he had hoped, but nobody figured on Badger.

That damned whiskey-runner was worse than a lobo wolf. He never gave up. Bria found out, too late, that Badger had friends all over the country, that anybody Badger was chasing better steer clear of ranches and towns. So be it, so it was! If Badger came after him now, it was all over but counting coup.

Rose made camp in a box canyon off a dry creek, set ash posts and strung barbwire off the wagon roll across the mouth; the bay team could graze free each day while she kept watch on top the ridge. She paced off her ranges and fixed a rest for rifle and arms; if somebody followed her father, she would shoot the way he taught her: aim for the belt buckle, knock him down, then finish him off. The Winchester .30-.30 carbine was made for her size; not too heavy, easy to load and clean, plenty of killing power. Her effective range was less than the heavier rifles favored by her father and her Uncle Jean, but nobody who knew Rose Bria cared to argue with her at three hundred yards.

She worried all through the week; on the sixth day she got so nervous that one of her terrible headaches started coming on, but she walked five hours in the night and drove the pain from her head. On the seventh morning she packed the wagon and put the bay team on short lines before going to the ridge; at eleven o'clock her father rode past without a glance. She watched his backtrail until twelve-thirty before running to camp, by then he had stacked the fence posts, wound the wire, and hitched the bay team to the wagon. He was black-faced with that sooty, greasy look he got after a week or two of roughing it with no place to wash. He shook his head. Rose shook hers.

"By god!" Bria said. "I'm beginning to think he never made it!"

His stomach ached, there wasn't a spoonful of fat left on him, he had to take his belt up another notch on the fifth day. It helped to know that Bria and the other rider were as dirty and itchy as he was, maybe worse because they had more livestock to handle. On the sixth day he argued with himself: stay or go? He voted to make a full week's stand, move out on the eighth morning. On the seventh morning he took a scan north and there the bastard was, come out of somewhere on the saddle horse, leading four others across the low ground toward the Big Foot trail. Faint dust blended with the mist and was lost in winter haze; it was no time to celebrate.

Badger rode off Sheep Mountain and made a bee-line north to Imlay, bought a one-way fare for paints and self, rode the next eastbound freight to Weta, made two big packs from his wagon supplies, bought more at the general store, and headed north. He made a sit-up camp beside a pond; next morning reached the big alkali flat where, off to the west, he had followed Bria's first trail. His hunch was growing; he had food for three weeks and a vague idea of what might occur. The hazy part was where Bria intended to dig the hole and pull it in after him and the other rider.

Everything went better with Bria back on the familiar wagon seat and Rose riding the saddle horse. Bria sent her north with the horses while he drove west by north through a network of creeks and draws, moving in and out like the marble in a child's maze game. He came finally to the big creek, solid ice now, where Rose waited; waved her on and followed through the curves and bends between the deepening banks until they passed through the brush choking the east loop arm into the cottonwood grove. An hour later the wagon, bows and top folded away, was hidden under the tarp; the horses were grazing in the trees, both loops were fenced shut, wires covered with brush. In the big dugout, Bria struck a match and lit the lamp; light made everything warmer. He looked around; Rose had done a fine job of unpacking and getting things cleaned up. Bria sighed happily:

"Sleep in a bed!"

"Cot."

"No matter, be warm."

"Father, how long we stay?"

"Past Christmas."

"Then go south?"

"By god yes!" Bria said. "We need some sunshine."

"We watch tonight, Father?"

"Tomorrow, Rose. Sleep tonight."

Badger moved so slowly that anyone watching must think him scared, crippled, or both; he never walked onto a hilltop or ridgeline, around a creek bend, across a flat, from shadow into light, before spending minutes, sometimes hours, searching the land ahead. He looked for tracks while making certain no one saw him. He wanted to follow Bria while staying far from Bria. Uncle Bad Knees swore that putting your feet on another man's footsteps was like carving your name on his belly with a dull knife; if the man had any sensitivity, no matter how far ahead he was, he would feel your feet on his heart. The way to follow was find the tracks, walk a half-circle, see if the tracks ran the same direction; keep casting out and back, run your man to earth. In winter, in the badlands, there were few safe places to hide. The best was a cutbank dugout, a warm hole under a thick dirt roof where with plenty of grub, wood and water, a man could last all winter. Badger gave himself until Christmas.

He found the wagon tracks in the maze of creeks and draws; lost them, cast patiently up and down until they reappeared; kept at the deadly slow game, five days before he reached that spot where bay team and wagon met five horses, all passed over a frozen sandbar into a creek bottom frozen solid between ten-foot cutbanks. Badger trailed slowly, scouting east and west, until the banks rose to fifteen feet; close-hobbled the paints in a side ravine and climbed the nearby hill. He had enough elevation to follow the cutbank shadow course of the creek as it ran north, made a sudden tight loop, and ran off southwest. Inside the loop he saw the tips of cottonwoods; straight-banked, deep, protected from wind and weather. If someone was camped in that loop, in a dugout, it could be somebody else going about private business. But who had business in the badlands with Christmas a week off? Still, he had to identify Bria, if Bria was there, be absolutely sure he had the right man.

Badger climbed off the hill and took the paints west, crossed the creek's southwest course below the loop, found a canyon two miles west that suited his purpose. He put the paints on long neck lines, chopped a water hole in the pond, slung his binoculars and shotgun, and began walking out the country east. He found a ridge ideally located, hid behind a serrated outcropping, and stopped living by clock, stomach and light. If somebody was in that loop, in a

dugout, they would maintain a guard watch. Where?
On top. Badger wrapped in his blanket and got
through the night; next morning saw the man sitting
a few feet back from the cutbank rim against an
earth-colored ledge that blended into the land so
closely the man, wearing earth-colored clothes, was
invisible until the binoculars caught the reflection of
light on one overshoe buckle. Scarf wrapped over
fur cap, tied under chin, washed and shaved, Bria
sat staring south across the badlands.

Run to earth, but how did he finish it? No water
fight here, no Big Muddy to drown foolish jockeys.
If Bria went south after Christmas, he would drive
his bay team hitched to his camp wagon, the other
rider leading the extra horses. But take away team,
wagon and horses; how would two men travel on
foot through the badlands in the dead of winter?
That gave Badger the answer to where he could
finish it. The answer to how must come.

Minutes before full dark he saw Bria hand-and-toe
down a notched pole to the staircase platform and
enter the dugout. Badger walked off the ridge into
the creek bottom, opened his black bottle, rubbed
Uncle Bad Knees' horse medicine on his coat and
mittens; went boldly upstream to the brush fence,
found the post set against the west bank, unwound
three wires and pulled them from the brush across
the creek. He pushed through the brush into the
cottonwoods and approached the first dark shape, one
of the smaller horses whose liquid eye gleamed as
his nostrils snuffed the mittens. Badger rubbed his
coarse winter coat, ducked under his neck, and met
the bay team, fine big horses come eagerly to sniff
him. Why not? What horse could resist Uncle Bad
Knees' romantic perfume; blended in the black bottle
were two drops of mink, one skunk, a pregnant
mare's urine, stud horse sweat, and other ingredients
his uncle would carry to the grave. Not that his uncle
denied the potion to anyone, but the pallbearers

who escorted him to the chalk bluff, dead and thus anointed, had to be strong men with stronger noses, richly deserving the friendship of Uncle Bad Knees, who wanted no violet sniffers at his funeral. Bay team, saddle horse, four extras—Badger seduced them all, held them in suck-nosed thrall while he lifted the wagon tarp and took halters, leadline, and a sack of oats. Lurching under his load, he lured them through the brush fence down the creek into the side ravine where he let them crowd around and bunt at his head and arms while he slipped halters over twitching ears, hooked up the leadline, shouldered the sack of oats, mounted the saddle horse, and led them west to his canyon camp.

He kept them on leadline while he chopped the water hole open, broke out the last bundle of hay, and measured the oats. He wolfed a quick meal while they ate and he packed, switched his saddle and bridle to Bria's roan, led his enlarged horse herd north from the canyon into the wind become a gale. He rode north and east, swung south with the wind at his back, puzzled through pitch-black night until he found a narrow canyon mouth and ascended it through a dozen sharp bends into a natural cup. Grass, puddle of ice under a frozen spring, cut at the upper end where the squeezed tail of the canyon sneaked out of the cup and ran away in the night. The wind was a whisper overhead, cold penetrated but could be softened with fire; no need for refinements, they'd not linger to count the growth rings in the petrified slabs sticking willy-nilly from the dull gray sand. Badger hobbled and neck-lined paints and strangers; rode the saddle horse up the trail that was barely wide enough for a thin horse, onto the plateau north of the cutbank creek. He crossed a mile of rough, rocky ground to a point northwest of the creek loop, hobbled the saddle horse in a ravine, and climbed to the top of the ridge. Daybreak gave him an angled field of vision; soon after he focused his binoculars and scraped the last irritating pebble from under his belly, Bria appeared beside the wagon, looked all around, and ran for the dugout ladder.

Bria burst inside, grabbed his rifle, whirled back to the open door as Rose sat up, wide awake.

"He got the horses!"

"Out there, now?"

"No, go on. I'll cover you."

Rose dressed, took her rifle with her from the dug-out into the grove. When she returned, her father was stacking cartridge boxes and food on the table beside the backpacks. Rose cooked breakfast while he filled the big canteen and changed certain important items of clothing. Socks, felt boots, overshoes, moccasins tied on the packs. Eating while Rose changed, Bria said,

"He sure wants us to chase him."

"Then stay here."

"Outlast him?"

"He's got to sleep, Father."

"How we know when, huh, cooped in here?"

"He can't hurt us."

Bria looked up. "Know what I'd do, I was him? Dynamite—blow the whole damn roof down on us. Didn't kill us in the blast, shoot us when we crawl out. No, by god! I ain't no rat in a hole."

"Trail him?"

"To start, not to finish. There's ways maybe even that smart sonabitch don' know."

"How we go?"

"Me first, you cover."

Badger watched them go down the creek, west out of sight up the side ravine; an hour later he saw two black dots move from his canyon camp, plod north on the wind-swept trail. Badger rode back to the canyon cup, found every horse asleep. He opened his pack, got a candle and a handful of kitchen matches, led the way south around the creek loop to the side ravine that brought them into the creek below the brush fence. He left the horses hobbled and tied, rode the saddle horse into the cottonwoods, tied him to a wagon wheel, took off his coat and mittens, and climbed the log ladder to the dugout door. He pushed it open with his shotgun barrel, counted ten before stepping inside, lighting his candle, finding himself in the best dugout he'd ever seen.

Cut from the soft, sandy rock, natural ceiling supported by upright posts wedged against long 2 x 8 stringers, natural fireplace in the back wall where the smoke rose through a hundred or more fissures that created a better flue than man could ' mortar. Cots, table, pots and pans, packs, sacks, cases. Badger started searching; stopped when he opened a battered shotgun shell case and found a can of black blasting powder, safety fuse, black insulating tape, crimper-cutter tool, and a shell box wrapped in an old shirt. He opened it and found a dozen blasting caps nested in cotton batting. Looking at the blasting powder, Badger thought of Bria, the other rider, and himself, in reference to time. How many more nights could they survive in the open? Each night cost them more reserve strength they could not restore with haphazard eating, long hours, and sleeping cold. Who would outlast the other? What was the sense in laying a trail to nowhere, going in circles until he, or they, outguessed the other and got the first shot?

Badger cut twenty feet of safety fuse from the roll, took it, the crimper-cutter tool, and the insulating tape down to the camp wagon. He found a folded nest of number-nine wire, straightened out fifteen feet, cut it, went up the log ladder to the notched pole, up the pole to the top above the dugout door. The dugout was five steps deep. Badger took five steps north, knelt, saw the fissures in the soft rock, blackened by the soot of many fires. He made an eyehook in one end of the wire and covered it with tape; pushed the wire, that end down, through the biggest fissure until it hit bottom. He cut off the spare wire six inches above the ground, twisted another eyelet, tied one end of the fuse into the eyelet, and taped both thickly. He stretched the fuse for easy pulling, went down into the dugout and found the taped wire end against the floor on the left side of the fire grate, less than an inch from the back wall. Badger pulled the wire down through the fissure, caught the taped fuse connection, pulled off the tape and untied the fuse, pulled it down another foot so that the end reached well past the center of the fire grate. He used his knife to dig the hole in the back wall, hole floor exactly level with the fireplace floor. He filled the hole with blasting powder, crimped a blasting cap to the fuse end, taped the crimp, and eased the cap and fuse into the powder charge. It took time to bury the fuse and cover the raw packed dirt, but after he had dusted, patted, and thumbed, he was satisfied that no one could see one speck of soot out of place. Last, he made five match torches of five matches each, taped securely together.

Badger blurred his own footprints as he backed from the fireplace, replaced every item in the shell case, carried the wound-up wire over one forearm, backed out of the dugout, closed the door, went up to the fuse end sticking out of the fissure, wound that into a tight little roll, eased it into the middle of the wire roll, and placed the wire over the fissure. He covered all signs with rock chips, dirt, and small stones, blurred his footsteps as he backed to the pole, went all the way down to the creek bed, ran to the wagon, put on his coat and mittens, rode downstream to the horses. The time, by sky and clouds and wind, was not yet past mid-morning. Badger led his herd south two miles, east away from the creek through ravines and over ridges to an alkali flat, north along the edge, west on a general line paralleling his east-bound trail three miles to the south. He stopped below a ridge, climbed up, and scouted the cutbank creek for sign of Bria. Too soon. He led the horses within half a mile of the dugout, shifted saddle and bridle back to the off paint, loosened the other paint's pack, hobbled all horses and put them on short neck lines. That was at noontime or a little later; within twenty minutes he was hidden on the rim of the cutbank creek, less than fifty steps across the north-east arc of the loop from the dugout door. He slept fitfully until late afternoon, woke to drink and chew hardtack, saw them come walking up the creek from the west-side ravine. They had followed his long trail all the way, stopped at the mouth of the ravine, saw the tracks mill, then go south, and made a sensible decision: get at least one more warm night's sleep, resume the chase in the morning. Badger watched them stop beside the wagon, talk a minute, go on up the log ladder into the dugout.

Waiting for darkness, Badger remembered all he knew about blasting powder. Slower than dynamite, it did not shatter like dynamite but gave a sort of heaving action, broke up the rock, coal, or dirt into big fragments. To give the best results, it had to be loaded right, balanced and carefully stemmed, but that took an expert. One thing most people did was use too much powder every time. Then night came and Badger walked painfully around to the fuse, un-covered it, removed the fuse from the wire, and used his knife to cut off the unneeded length eight inches from the fissure. Mittens off, he lay ear to the ground, listened and smelled. He wanted to light the fuse after their fire had burned down to hot coals and a few blue flames. The blast from the back wall hole should blow the fire all over the dugout, start small fires, fill the room with smoke, make them run out-side for air.

Could he pull the trigger?

Badger waited patiently, sitting with crossed legs around the fissure, fuse held in the sheltered pocket of thighs and body. He could smell smoke from his sitting position, he dare not wait longer. He pulled one bundle of matches from his coat pocket, gripped the fuse in his left hand, scratched the match heads on rock, held the flame to the fuse end until it sizzled and started on the trip. Badger shoved both mittens in his pockets, cradled his shotgun, moved to the rim of the cutbank about twenty steps east of the doorway. Approximately fifteen feet of fuse would take about ten minutes to burn down. His hands rubbed the ice-cold shotgun steel; waiting, counting, he was near exhaustion when it blew.

A dull thump shifted the ground under his feet, sparks flew upward from the fissures; then he heard, and felt deeply, the second explosion and knew he had used too much blasting powder in the back wall hole, that something had been blown the few feet across the dugout against the shell case, with enough sudden shattering effect to detonate the blasting caps, and the caps had exploded the whole can of blasting powder by propagation. The ground heaved up and down, the dugout door blew straight out over the creek and fell, trailing sparks, the entire roof of the dugout suddenly collapsed inwardly, upright posts danced briefly in the glare of a dozen fires, long stringers snapped into jagged pieces. Dust and flame and smoke rose up and mingled in the wind, nothing remained but the wooden door casing, standing alone, front walls and roof fallen around it.

Badger moved along the rim until he looked straight down into the smoke and fire, heard a groan that ended in a bubbling grunt. He knew that sound; somebody had just died down there. Someone else tried to speak but the throat seemed full, the best the mouth could manage was a groan. Then wind swirled down, blew the smoke away, the dust settled, and Badger saw her in the smashed, jagged opening, man's blue flannel shirt ripped away from her left arm and shoulder, showing the small breast and the gaping cut in the upper arm, trying to crawl upward through the debris, rifle in her right hand, lever down, action back, as if she got that far in loading when the blast came. She looked up and saw Badger at the moment he looked down and saw his mother's necklace around her neck.

11

Badger drove from Swiftwater to the cold, empty farm, north through the bare hills to the cabin on the oak bluff above the frozen river. Four-eyes came running from the cabin, leaped into his arms, licked his face and barked her welcome. He put the paints in the barn and followed her back to the cabin door, heard the familiar voice call harshly:

"Come in, nephew!"

Badger stepped inside, closed the door behind Four-eyes, looked at his uncle sitting in the same chair in the midst of the same pieces of life, blanket over his shoulders a reluctant concession to winter drafts. The old face fractured in that bittersweet smile.

"Nephew, you look terrible."

"Tired, Uncle."

"What's that stink?"

"Your horse medicine on my coat and mittens."

"Haugh, take 'em off—" and after Badger had put them in the corner "—nephew, you're thin as a matchstick, don't you know enough to eat?"

"No time, Uncle."

"How do you feel?"

"All right, Uncle, but I think I got a bad tooth."

"Go see the dentist."

"I'll go to Fairview, Uncle. Mike knows a good one."

His uncle looked as if he intended to smile, thought

better of a charitable act, and opened his peyote bag. Badger put the kettle on, waited until the tea steeped before taking the chair across the table and filling their cups. They drank and his uncle looked at him and shook his head in one small gesture. It was time. Badger took his mother's necklace from his shirt pocket and placed it on his uncle's hands. The fingers closed with gentle fierceness, the old eyes glowed.

"All dead?"

"All dead, Uncle." Badger took the sheaf of paper money from his other shirt pocket. "Eleven hundred dollars from the last two. They must of changed the gold into this after the race."

He waited for his uncle to say, "What gold?" but his uncle only drank tea and nodded. "The gold from your cache."

"You knew that, Uncle?"

"Your mother told me the day you started it. It always worried her. Maybe you better go down and put it back, huh?"

"Yes, Uncle."

"Build fires, drive the cold out. I'll come tomorrow. All the family will come."

"They know I'm home?"

"Louie was watching for you at the station. He will tell them. Four-eyes stays with me tonight. Tomorrow you can tell the story."

Badger went out and harnessed the paints, let them pick their way down the old trail off the oak bluff through the hills, across the north pasture into the barn. He unhitched and unharnessed, carried water, forked hay, ran to the house, lit the kitchen lamp, started a fire in the stove, set the lamp on the floor in the northeast corner, and got down beside the floorboard. He lifted it, dug the earth from the shaft, reached down, and felt the can. Fingers trembling, he brushed the dirt away and pulled the lid up. Full to the brim with double eagles, the lamplight reflected on his secret cache.

ABOUT THE AUTHOR

FRANK O'ROURKE was born in Denver, has lived in Europe and Mexico and now resides in California. He is the author of more than two dozen novels which include: *Bandolier Crossing, Battle Royal, Blackwater, The Diamond Hitch, The Professionals, The Swift Runner, The Shotgun Man* and *Badger*.

"REACH FOR THE SKY!"

and you still won't find more excitement or more thrills
than you get in Bantam's slam-bang, action-packed
westerns! Here's a roundup of fast-reading stories by
some of America's greatest western writers: